Why didn't he say something to her?

What was he checking for? Daniel Stewart, with his handsome, intelligent face and keen eyes, was indeed a man who would be hard to trick into believing that Lucy was her twin, Celia.

The silence was turning sinister and Lucy wanted to shout—you're not my type, never were! But that would blow her cover wide. "What's the matter?" she finally asked. "Why are you staring?"

"Sorry," he said, but his smile was unrepentant. Lucy took a deep breath, wishing she hadn't agreed to protect her sister, wishing she hadn't agreed to come.

But she was here. Being grilled by a smiling man with piercing eyes. A man who thought he'd slept with her in Cyprus, she thought hysterically. *Only it wasn't me...it was Celia!*

OTHER
Harlequin Romances
by JANE DONNELLY

No Way Out

by

JANE DONNELLY

Harlequin Books

TORONTO • LONDON • LOS ANGELES • AMSTERDAM
SYDNEY • HAMBURG • PARIS • STOCKHOLM • ATHENS • TOKYO

Original hardcover edition published in 1980
by Mills & Boon Limited

ISBN 0-373-02373-1

Harlequin edition published December 1980

Printed in U.S.A.

CHAPTER ONE

Lucy Friis backed her small van through the archway between the half-timbered buildings and into the yard. She had done well at the auction, the van contained several items of inexpensive wooden furniture, and after they were stripped and restored and painted each piece would make a healthy profit.

She went through the side door into the shop, smiled at a couple of possible customers who were inspecting a dove-grey chest of drawers, covered with a flight of painted bluebirds, and asked, 'Everything okay?' softly of Mrs Partridge, who was hovering hopefully behind them.

'You had a caller,' said Mrs Partridge.

That wasn't unusual. Lucy was running a business here, but this caller seemed to have put a sparkle into Mrs Partridge's mild blue eyes. She was looking quite roguish. 'He left you a note,' she said, nodding towards the office door.

The note was on the desk, held down by an ink bottle, and Lucy's eyebrows rose as she read it. 'I'm staying at the Crown. Is there any chance of you having dinner with me tonight, say seven o'clock? Daniel Stewart.'

The Crown was the best hotel in town, and a good place to discuss business or anything else, especially after dinner; but it would have helped if Daniel Stewart had stated his business. Lucy couldn't recall him, although she got around, buying and selling, and she had a fairly wide social life. She could have met him and forgotten the name.

She sat down, frowning and thinking. Perhaps it did

5

ring a faint bell. Stewart ... Stewart ... Daniel
Stewart ...

Mrs Partridge came in and announced glumly,
'They've gone off to think about it,' then she cheered
up, looking at the note. 'Pity you missed him,' she said.
She knew what was written there, a dinner invitation.

'Did he say what he wanted?' Lucy turned the piece
of paper over, although it was obvious there was nothing written on the back.

'Well, he wanted to see you.' Lucy had gathered that
much. 'I told him you were out and when you'd be
back, but he said he'd be out for the rest of the day
himself and did I by any chance know whether you'd
be free this evening.'

Friday evenings Lucy helped to pack up the goods
they would be taking to market tomorrow. Mrs Partridge knew that but considered it something that could
be managed without her. 'I told him you would,' she
said.

She and her husband had a special relationship with
Lucy. They had always been Aunt Dolly and Uncle
Joe, although there was no blood kinship, and for years
they had vetted her boy-friends. They were usually
hard to please, but Dolly Partridge seemed very taken
with this man.

'Who is he?' she wanted to know, and Lucy had to
admit,

'I haven't a clue.' Except for that feeling that she
ought to remember *something* about him. 'What did he
look like?'

'Not the sort of young man I'd have forgotten when
I was your age,' said Aunt Dolly, plump and sweet
and no longer young, but with an aura of contentment
about her. 'Very nice looking,' she added. 'Very nice
manners too.'

'Sounds a right charmer,' Lucy muttered, and Aunt
Dolly went on enthusiastically,

'Tall, brown hair—and a really nice smile. He seems

to know you.' Her glance settled once more on the note. 'Well, enough to be asking you out tonight.'

Lucy made a puzzled face, and Aunt Dolly made a knowing one, indicating that she wasn't born yesterday, but if Lucy wanted to keep quiet about this young man she would understand. Joe was always teasing, pretending that Lucy was letting the years slip by, and asking what was going to happen to the business if she didn't hurry up and find a husband, who could take over when Joe had to retire, and start a family to ensure the continuation of the firm. As though it was a nationwide affair instead of a workshed, a small shop, and a stall on the Friday market.

Joseph Partridge and Lucy's father had been partners, furniture restorers and dealers in bric-à-brac, never making much money but working happily together until Richard Friis's death when Lucy was in her final year at art college.

It had long been decided that when Lucy finished her Graphics course she would come into the shop, painting wooden furniture with her own original designs, and it was sad that things had not worked out just as they'd planned.

She couldn't take her father's place. She wasn't a cabinet-maker, but her bright imaginative young talent made her work more exciting than the Victorian restoration had ever been, and although they still sold small items of a bygone age the big sales now were mostly Lucy's work.

Joe stripped down and repaired the wooden furniture, getting it ready for Lucy to do the painting. Profits were rising steadily and Joe and Dolly were as proud of Lucy as her father would have been. She had always been like a daughter to them. As well as working here she spent more time in their cottage next door than she did in her mother's home. She had a bedroom here, up under the eaves, and it was a cosy, profitable and loving set-up.

Aunt Dolly went back into the shop, and Lucy sat staring at the note. If Daniel Stewart was all that striking she should be remembering him. Aunt Dolly wasn't usually over-impressionable. She looked a simple soul, in her unfashionable clothes, no scrap of make-up on her face, but she was nobody's dupe and here she was carrying on as though Robert Redford had strolled in and made a beeline for her.

Lucy opened the bottom drawer of the desk for the local phone directory, looked up the Crown and dialled the number. He had said he would be out for the rest of the day, but there was always a chance she might get him, or learn something about him.

What she did learn was what he did for a living. 'I believe you have a Mr Daniel Stewart staying with you,' she began, and the girl who answered said, 'Mr Stewart the photographer? He isn't in at the moment. Can I take a message?'

'I'll call again,' said Lucy. She whistled soundlessly as she replaced the receiver. If that was the explanation it could be rather awkward. She dialled another number, chewing her underlip as she waited for a reply. 'Lucy here,' she said, 'is Celia in?'

'It is Friday, you know,' said the woman who had answered, reproachfully.

'Sorry,' murmured Lucy. Her sister's housekeeper was a treasure but, like a lot of people around Celia, thought Lucy was a scatterbrain. She was always saying how strange it was that the two girls were sisters, let alone twins.

On Fridays, schedule permitting, Celia took the children over to have tea with Maman, her mother and Lucy's. It was the highlight of the week for Maman, just as Celia was the highlight of her life. Lucy knew that her mother loved her too, of course, but Celia was the daughter who was fulfilling all Maman's hopes and dreams.

Celia answered the phone this time, and it was like

Lucy's own voice talking to her. They were supposed to be identical, but Celia was the beauty although they had the same features. Lucy laughed more. She was going to have laugh lines before she was much older, she was twenty-two now, but Celia would probably be smooth skinned all her life.

The differences were under the skin, and although the two girls got along very well together their personalities differed sharply. Celia had been a dainty exquisite child while Lucy was climbing trees, and helping on farms, and coming home looking, as Maman would say shuddering, like a gutter urchin.

Maman was French by birth. She still used words you might read but that nobody actually said, as though even after twenty-five years she still was not quite at home here.

But Celia made up for everything. The girls started art school together, and were probably equally talented, but while she was still a first-year student Celia had married one of the most eligible men in town, the young local M.P., no less, and made him a wonderful wife.

It was a complete success. Celia never put a foot wrong, she charmed everyone voters, colleagues. Like the young Kennedys the Clendinnens seemed to have everything in their world going for them.

'Hello,' said Celia.

'I've just come back from Pewters' Auction,' said Lucy, 'and sombody called Daniel Stewart has been in the shop asking for me. He left a note, he's at the Crown and will I have dinner with him tonight. I don't think I know a Daniel Stewart, but he's a photographer, and wasn't that the name of that photographer you met last year in Cyprus?'

There was silence, as though Celia was trying to remember too. Then she said, 'Yes, yes, it was.'

'Well, what does he want with me?'

Another silence. 'I talked about my family,' Celia

said at last, and Lucy had the impression that she was holding the phone close, her head bowed and a hand cupped over the mouthpiece so that she could speak very quietly. 'Can you get over here?' she asked softly, confirming the suspicion that she didn't want anyone overhearing her. 'Come and have tea with us,' she added with a spurious gaiety. 'Come right away.'

'I think I'd better.' Lucy wasn't liking the sound of this. About twelve months ago Celia had been run down. There had been a general election. It was a safe seat, Howard was a sure winner, but of course there had been a lot of work and stress for the Member's wife and afterwards her doctor had suggested a few days of rest and sunshine. Howard had fixed up a surprise holiday for her, at an hotel in Cyprus. She had gone along alone and returned relaxed and blooming.

A little while afterwards she had told Lucy about meeting a charming man, a photographer called Daniel Stewart, on her last but one evening. They had had dinner together, and gone sightseeing next day, and Celia had laughed and confessed, 'It's a good job I've got old-fashioned ideas about marriage.'

Lucy had laughed too and thought no more about it. But the only reason Daniel Stewart would come looking for Lucy would be Celia. As she was married to a man in the public eye, where a hint of scandal could be damaging, he might have had scruples about a direct contact. He must have thought Celia had told Lucy about him, that Lucy might say how the land lay, even perhaps act as a go-between.

It was twelve months ago, and it was nothing but a few hours spent with a holiday companion, but Celia did have a devastating effect on men. The sisters shared the same delicate features, fair hair, heart-shaped face, small tip-tilted nose and wide clear eyes. But Lucy had a way of lifting her head, and setting her jaw, that took some of the fragility away from her. It was Celia who would have broken hearts, if she hadn't married Howard. Since then there had never been any question of anyone but him.

She mixed with other men, of course. She flirted with them and fascinated them, but Howard had a possessive streak and Celia knew exactly where to stop.

Lucy dropped the note into her handbag, and went into the shop to tell Aunt Dolly she would be out for the next hour or so. Aunt Dolly probably thought that Lucy was off to buy herself a new dress, or get her hair fixed.

'Take your time,' she said happily, and would be surprised a couple of minutes later to see Lucy's van—still with its small load of furniture—passing the window.

The family home was in a village about four miles away and Lucy was soon drawing up in front of a neat Victorian house, with a carefully tended front garden. Maman was a tidy lady. No weeds grew in her herbaceous borders and no greenfly nibbled her standard rose bushes.

Celia came through the front door, as Lucy got out of her van and reached Lucy at the gate, smiling and linking arms with her. 'I'm so glad you could get over,' said Celia. It was two or three weeks since the sisters' last meeting; they both led busy lives.

Their similarity was not striking at first sight. Lucy looked slightly skinnier, she was a few pounds lighter, and Celia was better dressed, better groomed. Often the twin-resemblance had to be pointed out before people said, 'My goodness, yes!'

'Maman's playing with Melanie,' said Celia, guiding Lucy round the side of the house into the back garden, which was mostly lawn and trees. Melanie was four years old, and Roland, the longed-for son aged two months, was in his pram under a weeping willow.

Lucy went across to look in on him. He was sleeping and quite beautiful, and she resisted the temptation to

hug and kiss and disturb his slumber. Coming round
the house Celia had been chattering about the lovely
hot weather. Now they were away from the house, in
the middle of the lawn, she asked abruptly, 'Who saw
him? What did he say exactly?'

'He spoke to Aunt Dolly,' said Lucy, and Celia
shuddered fastidiously, a habit she shared with Maman.

'That old gossip!'

'No, she is not,' Lucy protested hotly. 'She likes to
know what's going on, but she isn't a gossip.'

'What did he *say*?'

Lucy straightened, from bending over the baby's
pram, to look closely at Celia, who didn't sound as
though she was hearing about someone she hardly
knew. More as though Lucy was the bearer of bad news
and she was bracing herself for the worst.

'He asked if I was around,' Lucy said slowly. 'Then
he asked if Aunt Dolly knew if I was free this evening,
and then he left a note.'

'Did you bring it?'

Lucy produced the **single** sheet and Celia pounced
on it, scanned the few lines, and crumpled the paper
into a small ball held tightly in her fist.

'I gather you don't want to renew the acquaintance,'
Lucy said drily.

'*No*, I do *not*!' She couldn't remember Celia sounding as emphatic as this about anything. Celia never
seemed to have very strong views. She believed in
what Howard believed in, his politics and his party,
but she never did any fierce arguing. She never seemed
to dislike people either, even when she disapproved of
them. But from the way she was crushing that scrap of
paper there would be no welcome for Daniel Stewart,
for all her glowing description of him when she came
back from her holiday in Cyprus.

'Very well,' said Lucy. 'We ignore him.'

Of course she wouldn't be having dinner with a total
stranger. She would ignore the note and the man. If

he turned up in the shop again she would be chilly. Celia rocked the pram gently with the hand that wasn't clutching the note and asked, 'Did he say how long he was here for?'

'I don't think so. Aunt Dolly didn't say anything about that. She was very struck with him, though. She said he was very handsome.'

'He is.' Celia was looking at the baby as if they were talking about him, and Lucy recapped,

'Sitting at the next table to you, and then you knocked over a glass of wine, and you both laughed and started talking and finished your meal at the same table. And went sightseeing together next day.'

'Yes.' Celia was still rocking the pram, her long dark lashes making a shadow on her flushed cheeks as she said very softly, 'But, you see, that wasn't all we did together.'

Lucy couldn't have been more astonished. With most girls she would have been prepared for that twist to the story, but not with Celia. Thousands of miles from home, all alone in such a romantic setting, most women might lose their heads for a while. But in Celia it seemed as out of character as a confession of murder, scattering Lucy's wits so that for a moment she actually stared at the baby, gasping, and Celia shrieked, 'No!'

Roland was born ten months after that holiday, but this had shaken Lucy profoundly. It took her the best part of a minute to pull herself together enough to ask, 'Well, what do we do? I can see why you don't want him calling round, although I don't think Howard would suspect in a million years.'

At the thought of her brother-in-law she winced, because Howard was one of the nicest of men, and he adored Celia. But he did see things in black and white, and Lucy dared not imagine how he would react if he ever found out about this.

'This man isn't the blackmailing type, is he?' she croaked.

'Oh no.' Celia seemed sure, and that was something to be thankful for, but Lucy was deeply shocked. And disappointed, because she had always thought that Celia was as happy and perfect a wife and mother as anyone could ever find anywhere.

She was in a state of stupefied disbelief. If Celia had had a crazy sense of humour—like Lucy's own—she would have waited for her to giggle and say, 'Fooled you, didn't I? You should see your face!' But Celia was looking sick with worry, and Lucy gulped and said briskly, 'Then phone him up at the Crown and say hello and goodbye, and make it a definite brush-off.'

'Yes, I will.' Celia's voice was very low, and got lower until Lucy had to strain to hear. 'But if he should turn up again at the shop,' said Celia in a husky whisper, 'I said I was you.'

'You did *what*?' Lucy yelped, and Celia turned away from the pram and walked quickly across the lawn to the farthest point from the house, where a walnut tree grew in the corner. Under that, long ago, their father had built a wooden bench.

Celia sat down on the bench and Lucy, just behind her, asked hoarsely, 'What on earth possessed you to do that?'

'I don't know.' Celia's smooth pretty face was puckered. 'I suppose I didn't want to be married for an hour or two. I didn't want to say, "I'm Mrs Howard Clendinnen, mother of a three-year-old." I just wanted to be free and on holiday and chatting up this fantastic man.'

Lucy had sat down too, her knees had given way, and it seemed reasonable to demand, 'Then why weren't you Celia Smith? You didn't have to give him my name.'

'I tell you I don't *know*,' Celia wailed. 'Honestly, it came out before I had time to think, and of course he could have found out who I was easily enough. But I just said your name, and then I talked about your work and your shop and your market stall.'

The corners of her lips began to lift slowly, as though she knew she shouldn't be smiling but she couldn't help it. 'It was fun,' she said softly. 'The best part of the holiday. I'd taken it easy all week, swimming in the pool, sitting in the sun—on my own mostly. I'd spoken to other people, of course, but nothing personal, and then this incredibly attractive man turned up at the next table and we hit it off right away.'

'It sounds like it,' said Lucy wryly. 'You did sleep with him? That is what you're saying?'

Celia answered with a silent nod.

'Still using my name? Thanks very much! You might have warned me.'

'He was off to Cambodia or somewhere like that, and it was just a holiday affair.' Celia produced her excuses. 'We said goodbye—you know, really goodbye. I never expected to see him again. I didn't give him an address or a phone number or anything.'

Then she admitted, biting her lip, 'Although I did say I lived in the Cotswolds, and I suppose I might have mentioned Moreton Meadows.'

'And you said you made hand-painted furniture, and had a shop and a stall on the market, and your name was Lucy Friis,' Lucy snapped, exasperated. 'He wouldn't need to be Sherlock Holmes to track that down. You'd better phone and say you won't be meeting him for dinner. Or for anything else.'

'Oh, I will, yes,' said Celia fervently. 'But if he should come round to the shop again you will back me up?'

'Say it was me?' Lucy looked down at her long legs in paint-spattered jeans, and at Celia in shell-pink strap sandals and silk chiffon dress in muted greys and rose, and hooted derisively, 'He'll know it wasn't.'

'No, he won't.' Suddenly there was an urgency in Celia's voice, bordering on desperation. '*Please*, Lucy! He wouldn't know. I looked more like you out there than I've ever done. I wasn't bothering. I'd got my hair loose.' Her fingers brushed the smooth golden chignon as though she would ruffle it to show how it could be identical to Lucy's bright flyaway mop. 'I was a bit thinner too. I've put that back on since.'

'Did you tell him you had a twin?'

Celia rubbed her forehead as though she was struggling to remember. 'No, I'm sure I didn't. I only said I had a married sister,' and Lucy sighed deeply.

'Very well then. If he does walk in I'll freeze him off.' She went on looking worriedly at her sister. 'But I don't know. I don't understand any of this. It doesn't sound a bit like you.'

'Of course it wasn't like me.' Celia's pink cheeks flushed deeper and she turned away with quivering lips. 'Don't you think I'm ashamed of myself? Do you think I don't know it was a terrible thing to do?'

Incredible. Unbelievable. It made Celia suddenly a stranger, because Lucy would have sworn that her sister had never given another man a second thought, much less actually taken one as a lover. She asked apprehensively, 'You don't make a habit of this kind of thing, do you?' but Celia's ringing indignation was reassuring.

'Of course I don't! How can you ask that? Of course it was the first time and it will be the last. It was just a crazy fling.' She shook her head in dazed bewilderment. 'I can't believe it myself. I can't believe it happened. I'd forgotten it, I really had. It's the sort of thing that might happen to you but never to me.'

'I don't go hopping into bed with strangers,' snapped Lucy, and Celia caught her sister's hand, squeezing it hard, apologising.

'Lucy, I'm sorry. I didn't mean that the way it sounded. But you are a free agent, aren't you, and you've never taken life as seriously as I have.'

A small girl, with fat flaxen curls, came out of the house, shrieking 'Tea's ready!' then, spotting Lucy, the shriek rose higher, 'Aunt Lucy!' and she flew across the lawn like a bird, arms wide. Lucy jumped up, and caught her, and whirled her round and round.

'Don't get her too hot,' said Celia in faint reproof, as their mother emerged from the kitchen door and added her voice.

'Melanie dear, don't make so much noise!' The child was squealing with delight. 'Lucy, don't over-excite her'.

Lucy put the little girl down and knelt in front of her, brushing back the curls that had tumbled over her face. 'She can stand a bit of rough and tumble, can't you, Melly? She's a toughie.'

'She's her grandmamma's little lady,' said Maman, 'and she's lost her hair ribbon.' A blue ribbon, that had been tied in an Alice band, had slipped off on to the grass, and Lucy retrieved and replaced it. 'What brought you home?' Maman asked. Friday nights Lucy usually slept over the shop to be ready for early rising next morning. Saturday was market day.

'I told you,' said Celia. 'She just phoned to speak to me and I asked her. It is over a fortnight since we've seen each other.'

'I'm sure Lucy could manage to get round to see you in the evenings if she tried,' said Maman, and Lucy knew there was no point in arguing that she probably worked much harder than Celia. Celia had two children and, as the local M.P.'s wife, was in constant social demand. But she did have a devoted household staff and a very generous husband, and Lucy thought ruefully, anybody who looked at the pair of us could pick out the wage slave.

She knew that Maman wanted Celia, and the children, all to herself on Friday afternoons. Anybody else was intruding, even Lucy, and now Maman put her hand through Celia's arm and reached for Melanie, trailing the child along behind her across the lawn.

They made a pretty picture, the elegant women, the

beautiful child. Celia had always been closest to
Maman, just as Lucy had been her father's girl. If anything should happen to rock Celia's marriage it would
just about kill Maman, and Howard would take adultery very hard. His own mother had left his father for
another man when Howard was a boy, and Howard was
still bitter about that. He had put Celia on a pedestal
and her excuses—that this had only been a holiday
fling and she never expected to see Daniel Stewart
again—wouldn't impress him.

They didn't reassure Lucy much. She still felt in
almost total shock. None of this sounded like Celia,
but it had happened, and Daniel Stewart was in town,
looking for 'Lucy Friis' with whom he had had a brief
but enjoyable affair. Celia was ashamed of herself,
but she had smiled, remembering, and Lucy had caught
herself wondering if Daniel Stewart had been a better
lover than good old Howard.

Inside the house she said, 'I don't think I'll stay for
tea after all, I've got a lot of work waiting at the
shop, I just wanted to see you and have a word with
you. You will make that phone call, won't you?'

Maman's face brightened, her happy hour with Celia
was on again, hearing all that Celia had done in the
past week, over the tiny cakes and the dainty sandwiches.

'Of course I will,' Celia said quickly, and Lucy kissed
them all, with an extra hug for Melanie, who was
wailing,

'Where are you going, Aunt Lucy?'

'I'll come and see you soon,' Lucy promised. Maman
would be curious about this phone call, and Celia
would probably pretend it was business—perhaps a
friend of hers wanting some of Lucy's work. Several
of Lucy's pieces were in Celia's home, and they got
admired. Commissions had come her way before
through them.

She drove back to the shop and began to unload the

van, being joined almost at once by Joe Partridge. A lanky leather-faced sixty-year-old, he was in working gear, a heavy twill navy blue apron, and shirt sleeves rolled up; and he did most of the unloading, grunting approval from time to time. 'Nice piece. How much? You did well there.'

Lucy usually did well at sales. She knew what she should pay and what she was looking for. Not the real antiques, which it would have been sacrilege to paint over, but sound second-hand furniture in attractive shapes.

Everything was stocked in an outbuilding, except for a couple of small side tables that Joe took into the workshed. Small tables were a quick seller, as many as Lucy could paint. She was working on a dining table now, an order that was something of a rush job, and as soon as the van was empty she garaged it and then followed Joe into the workshed.

He was smoothing the surface of a small dresser that he had stripped down to the natural wood, sanding it with glass paper; and Lucy took her blue cheesecloth smock off one of the hooks behind the door, slipped it on, and went over to her own working spot by the window.

Uncle Joe wasn't much of a talker. He could go happily all day, exchanging little more than grunts and nods and the occasional little joke, but he was a wise old bird and Lucy always relied on him for help and advice. But this problem was different, she couldn't consult him on this. Neither could she tell Aunt Dolly. Nor any of her friends, because most of them would be tickled pink to hear that Celia the paragon had toppled off her pedestal.

This problem was all Lucy's, and she dipped her brush into a tiny pot of paint, and tried to forget it for a while and concentrate on the job in hand.

The table was round, on an octagonal pedestal, painted pale green with the letters D. E. monogrammed in the centre, and a pattern of elm leaves running round the edge. It was for a girl called Doreen Elms, a surprise present for her birthday ordered by her husband—whose name was Denis, so the monogram suited them both—and Lucy had enjoyed working on it until now.

But now she found her attention wandering and her hand none too steady. She was really shaken up. She had considered herself almost unshockable. It was a funny old world and there were some funny folk in it, but so long as they hurt nobody what folk got up to was their own business. Lucy was modern and broadminded and tolerant. She had her own moral standards, and she lived by them, and she didn't pass judgment on others.

But *Celia*... The idea of Celia having even the fleetest of holiday flings had stunned her. If she hadn't heard it from Celia herself she would never have believed it. Nobody would. But nobody else must be told, because once a whisper like that got around it would run like a lit fuse, reaching Howard at last, and then the powder keg would go up.

Howard idolised Celia. He had from their first meeting, which was at the annual church fête, opened by Howard as the very new very young M.P. He had been about twenty-eight then, earnest and pleasantly ugly, with a swarm of admiring women buzzing around him.

Celia was selling raffle tickets. Lucy had been helping in the tea tent, in charge of the urn, Maman was on the cake stall, and when Howard Clendinnen, bachelor M.P., and his entourage, came into the tea marquee, Celia was on his arm.

It must have been one of the proudest and happiest moments of Maman's life. Howard had bought all Celia's tickets and afterwards claimed that although he didn't win the hamper of groceries he certainly won the prize of his life. That was Celia.

In those days her current date was a nice boy who

worked in his father's hardware store, and Maman was terrified that Celia might marry into 'trade.' That had always sent Lucy into fits of giggles. They had a shop themselves, and surely nobody in the last fifty years, except Maman, talked about being 'in trade'. But in those days their mother was passionately concerned that Celia should marry well. She sometimes pointed out that she, personally, had married beneath herself, and although Lucy and her father usually grinned at each other when Maman was in a martyred mood Lucy always felt a flare of indignation because her father was such a good man.

Maman loved him, there was no doubt about that. She made him a caring wife, she nursed him devotedly and mourned him deeply; but on the day that Celia married Howard Clendinnen Maman was as radiant as the bride.

'Look at your mother,' Richard Friis murmured to Lucy. 'Now her prayers for Celia are answered I hope she won't start worrying about who you're going to marry.'

Lucy had been chief bridesmaid, collecting compliments and admirers, but she knew that Maman had never been as involved in Lucy's life as she was in Celia's. 'Not me,' Lucy had whispered back. 'I'm going to finish my course and then—pardon the expression—I'm thinking of going into trade.'

They had chuckled together, and he had said, 'She's got one daughter fixed up with an M.P. She can't expect to win 'em all.'

Maman loved being an M.P.'s mother-in-law, and Howard was considerate and kind, especially after Richard Friis's death. Lucy was very fond indeed of Howard. It hurt her to think of him being hurt, and not just hurt but completely shattered.

Howard was a happy family man, it *was* a happy family, and how Celia could have put it at risk was beyond Lucy. He was still a back-bencher, he probably never would be a high-flyer, but the Clendinnens were popular locally and often interviewed as an ideal family for newspapers and magazines. Maman cut out the clippings for her scrapbooks, and the house was full of photographs that had accompanied the articles, usually taken in their home or garden with the children.

But if Celia hadn't been bothering with her appearance, when she was holidaying in Cyprus, Daniel Stewart wouldn't have recognised her from any press photographs he might have come across. Celia would never allow a camera near unless she was bandbox-neat. Even when she was playing with the children her hairstyle and make-up were flawless, and her clothes were always haute couture.

Lucy gave a little cry of annoyance as her brush skidded and the leaf she was painting developed an added splodge. She reached quickly for a rag, and Uncle Joe looked up, from his rhythmic back-and-forth smoothing action, to ask, 'Anything wrong?'

'I slipped, that's all.'

'All, is it?'

'What else?'

It was all right, it had left no mark, but she wasn't producing her best work, and when Uncle Joe said, 'Seems to me you're doing a lot of sighing,' she straightened, startled. She hadn't realised her worry was showing.

'You know,' she said, 'I think I'm getting a headache. There was a real crowd at that auction. I think I'll go into the shop for a while.'

The workshed always smelt of stripper and paint and varnish. Acrid odours mingled in here, and strangers often started coughing. If Lucy was getting a headache she would be better in the pot-pourri atmosphere of the shop. 'Get yourself a strong cup of tea,' Uncle Joe advised.

'I'll bring you one out,' Lucy promised.

What was left of the afternoon, after making the tea, she spent in the shop, talking to tourists who had walked in to look round, selling some bric-à-brac and two painted windowboxes.

Aunt Dolly had gone into the cottage, to prepare the evening meal that she and Joe often shared with Lucy, when the phone rang in the office, just before six o'clock.

It was Celia. 'Lucy?'

'Yes.'

'I can't get him.' Celia's voice was shrill. 'I've been trying ever since I got home, and I've tried again just now, and he's still out, and if I just leave a message that I won't be turning up for dinner that isn't going to stop him coming round to the shop tomorrow, is it?'

'Probably not,' Lucy agreed. 'But he's bound to be at the Crown before seven o'clock. Tell him you're out of town for the next few days. Unless he's very thick-skinned that message ought to get through.'

Celia was probably using the phone in the bedroom, with the door closed, because she wasn't bothering to keep her voice down. 'I'm expecting Howard home any minute,' she wailed, 'and we're due at the Rotary dinner-dance tonight. I won't have a chance to go on phoning, so *please*—will you?'

Lucy wanted to wash her hands of the whole affair. She wanted to hear no more about it and pretend it had never happened, then perhaps it wouldn't be long before she could stop believing that it had.

'Can't you——' she began desperately. She was going to say, 'send him a note,' which would have been a lunatic thing to do, but her voice trailed off and Celia said,

'What? Can't I what?'

'I've no idea,' Lucy admitted helplessly, and Celia yelped,

'That's the car! Howard's home. Lucy, please—oh God, please, Lucy, ring up and tell him you can't meet him. Stop him coming. Stop him phoning. What am I going to *do*?'

Celia was usually such a placid girl. It was terrible to hear her going to pieces like this, and Lucy said, 'All right, all right, don't get into such a state. You haven't cut anyone's throat.'

'I feel as though I have,' Celia moaned. 'I feel so sick with myself I feel like cutting my own throat.'

'Yes, well, you were an idiot.'

'I couldn't help it. It wasn't my fault.'

Lucy's lips parted to say, 'He didn't rape you, did he?' but she held back the words because Celia seemed in no state for that kind of talk. 'All right,' she capitulated, 'I'll ring him.'

'Oh Lucy, Lucy, I love you!'

'I know,' said Lucy. 'And you should. Now stop fretting and go along and wow the Rotarians. And thank your lucky stars you've got Howard and the children.'

It was as well there was no one in the shop because the office door was open, but it was a few minutes after six now and Lucy went to the front door to turn the CLOSED notice, lock up, and pull down the blind. She hung around, tidying, for another fifteen minutes or so, and then tried ringing the Crown again.

Daniel Stewart was still out, and the girl at reception was remembering the voice as a vaguely familiar one that had already made a number of calls. Lucy guessed that Celia had become progressively more frantic because, when she asked for Mr Daniel Stewart, her voice so very like Celia's, the girl said, 'I'm awfully sorry, but he's still not back,' and sounded quite sympathetic.

'Thank you,' said Lucy cheerfully. She didn't want anyone deciding that a little local drama was being played out around a man who had just booked into the Crown. He might even have asked when he arrived if they could direct him to Lucy Friis's shop and, given the name, the girl in reception might recognise the voice.

This was a smallish town. Most of the natives knew each other. During the summer season the hotels took on holiday help, but in reception at the Crown, the staff usually stayed the same.

Blow this, thought Lucy, this is ridiculous. She dropped a notebook into the drawer of the desk and banged the drawer to, working herself up into righteous anger. Celia had no right to give Lucy's name to a casual pickup. What did that make Lucy out to be? It was an appalling thing to do, unforgivable.

And it would be unforgivable if Howard ever found out just what Celia had done, because he wouldn't forgive. The marriage might continue, he had his image with the voters to consider, but the foundation of their family life would be undermined for ever.

That was how Howard was. In politics he probably connived and dissembled with the rest of them, but he was basically loyal and honest and he would bitterly resent his wife giving herself to another man. Who wouldn't? Howard had an implacable streak. His mother had been dead for ages, but he still went tight-lipped if anyone mentioned her. 'That woman,' he called her. Oh, Celia would pay if he found out that she had cheated on him, and Lucy's anger on her own behalf shrivelled and died, because most of all she was scared for Celia. And for Maman.

This was a perilous situation. The man might talk. He might easily say to somebody, 'I met Lucy Friis in Cyprus last year,' and if they knew her they might say, 'I didn't know she went to Cyprus. Surely that was her twin, Celia, our M.P.'s wife.'

She began shivering, huddling in her chair. She hoped Celia wouldn't get these kind of thoughts tonight, while she was sitting at the top table as one of the guests of honour. If Celia looked upset Howard would be leaning solicitously across to her, and all the women would sympathise because it was only two months since she had had her baby. Although if they heard about Daniel Stewart they'd soon start counting on their fingers.

How long would he be staying here? Lucy wondered. If she asked him that, when she said she couldn't see him tonight, he'd think she was wondering when she could see him, he'd take it as encouragement.

What could she say on the phone that would make sure he didn't bother 'Lucy Friis' again? Something pretty drastic, like telling him she was married or engaged, but she discarded that idea at once. She couldn't have rumours like that floating around.

Anyhow, it was twelve months since Daniel Stewart and Celia had met, and there had obviously been no phone calls or letters, so he shouldn't be too surprised by a cool reception. It was happening all the time, holiday lovers meeting back home and being disappointed in each other; and he had let a whole year go by before he came looking for 'Lucy,' so he wasn't over-eager.

But if the brush-off was by phone curiosity might still bring him along to the shop, once more, to get a glimpse of her. And if he met Aunt Dolly again, and if she asked him where he and Lucy had met, well Aunt Dolly would certainly remember which sister had been to Cyprus.

So he had to be kept away from the shop, and if Lucy could find the nerve perhaps her best plan might be to turn up at the Crown. He wouldn't remember how Celia looked as vividly as though he had seen her recently, and physically they were identical twins.

She could turn up as Lucy Friis—she *was* Lucy Friis—and act as though the holiday affair had meant nothing much to her, and she wasn't much impressed by Daniel Stewart now she was seeing him again. Then, after a few minutes, she could say goodbye with the situation cooled and defused.

Lucy had always been impetuous. Celia was supposed to be the prudent one, although she hadn't shown much discretion in Cyprus, but Lucy was the girl for action. Perhaps she didn't always look before she leapt, although she thought she was thinking this out as calmly as she could, and she did hate hanging around. If there was a problem she was much happier doing something about it, and surely the obvious thing to do now was to go over to the Crown, just before seven o'clock, and face up to this Daniel Stewart and see him off.

Once she had decided on that she could leave the phone, and she went through the dividing door into the cottage, tracking down Aunt Dolly in the kitchen.

Dolly Partridge was in her element, serving up food. She was a born cook, an artist with the herbs that she grew in her small herb garden, and with every country recipe imaginable stored in her mind.

She never seemed to need a cookbook, but it was hard to find a dish that Aunt Dolly couldn't produce, and surprising how many exotic chef's specials were derived from traditional recipes. Considering how well she fed Uncle Joe it was astonishing that he never put on extra weight. Lucy remembered him always the way he was now, tough and stringy, but he ate as well as any man in town.

'That smells good,' said Lucy, as Aunt Dolly gave a final rosemary and redcurrant basting to a small roast of lamb, and Aunt Dolly said smugly,

'You won't get better at the Crown.'

'I know that.' Lucy put condiments on the table that was part-laid for two. 'And I doubt if I'll be eating at the Crown anyway. This man, I've been trying to remember where I could have met him, and I think it might have been on holiday somewhere. But if he's who I think he is he was an awful bore. I'm sure I can remember that, and I doubt if I'll want to be stuck with him for hours.'

'You don't say,' said Aunt Dolly, as though she didn't believe a word of it. 'Fancy that!' She shut the oven door and smiled, 'Now I'd have put him down as being a young man who would be very good company. Just shows, doesn't it, you never can tell.'

The smile was broad, and for the life of her Lucy couldn't meet the twinkling eyes, although Aunt Dolly's suspicions were a mile off the mark.

'You'll be going home to get changed, I suppose,' said Aunt Dolly, and Lucy hesitated. She had just about time enough, but if she left here Daniel Stewart might decide to stroll over, or phone; and now Aunt Dolly's curiosity was whetted, and Lucy was providing no answers, she would certainly grab the chance to get in a few questions.

'I'll freshen up here,' Lucy decided.

She kept a few clothes in the bedroom under the eaves. Not her best, but something to change into if she stayed overnight. She wasn't dressing to impress and she chose a short-sleeved little yellow cotton shirt-waister that she had bought off the market a couple of weeks ago.

It was a warm evening, she didn't need a jacket when she strolled into the high street and along towards the Crown. This had been quite a day. In a few weeks— well, perhaps a few months, she was going to look back on today and wonder if she had dreamed it all. Celia, with a secret lover, was mind-boggling. I shall never understand, Lucy thought, never.

The only way she could explain her sister acting so completely out of character was that Celia must have had a kind of running-wild brainstorm. Had she never worried about this man turning up? She hadn't even mentioned him until—it must have been about three months after she came back from the holiday, and even

then she hadn't warned Lucy that she'd used her name.
So that Lucy would have been prepared if he should
have arrived on her doorstep. As he had. All that Celia
had said was that they'd gone sightseeing together, and
he was fantastic and it was a good thing she had old-
fashioned ideas about marriage. All this sitting in her
beautiful drawing room, with the trappings of the
good life around her, waiting for Roland.

Howard had always wanted a son. Now they were the
perfect family, and one mistake—because that was
what it was, one crazy lapse—wasn't going to spoil all
the years ahead if Lucy could help it. She walked faster,
anxious to get to this man, say her piece, and get away
again, and within a few minutes she reached his hotel.

The Crown had been a coaching inn in the old days,
the cobbled stone courtyard entrance hadn't changed
much, and the foyer was still oak-panelled with a wide
staircase curving to the upper floors.

Behind the reception desk a young woman was on
the phone, looking cool and competent, assuring somebody that what they were asking for could be supplied,
and making a note at the same time. Lucy stood waiting, and the receptionist looked up and gave her a
smile that widened.

Lucy knew Carole Whittaker. When Carole replaced
the pone she said, 'Mr Stewart is in the Falstaff Bar.
He said if you came would I ask you to go through.
Lucky you,' she added in lowered tones.

'Thanks,' said Lucy. Mr Stewart didn't lack for admirers—everybody seemed to fancy him, including
Aunt Dolly if she had been younger—and Lucy was
curious to see him.

She went through the archway that had Falstaff Bar
emblazoned above it. All the public rooms were named
after Shakespearean characters. The small coffee lounge
upstairs was called The Merry Wives, as though nobody else drank coffee. At this time of an evening, and
this time of year, the bars were fairly full, and Lucy

stood in the entrance, looking around.

She hadn't thought about that, that she ought to know him when she saw him. Aunt Dolly had said that he was good-looking, tall with brown hair; but that description could have been loosely applied to several of the men who were seated around the tables or standing at the bar.

How was she going to explain not recognising him? 'Sorry, I'm terribly shortsighted.' 'Sorry, I've got a rotten memory.'

Then she saw him and she knew.

He was coming towards her and he was one of the most strikingly handsome men she had ever seen. It was the kind of face Renaissance artists loved to paint, with flared nostrils and sombre eyes, arrogant as the devil. Young men who believed they had inherited the earth.

Lucy had never been partial to very handsome men. Nor, come to that, to women whose faces could have been their fortune. Not that she knew many of the Beautiful People, but the spectacular lookers she had come across usually seemed to be in love with themselves and had very little consideration left over for lesser mortals.

Right now the eyes of at least half the women in the Falstaff Bar were following Daniel Stewart. He began to smile just before he reached Lucy, showing beautiful white teeth, and she thought—he thinks he's God's gift; and dislike rose in her so that all she wanted to do was turn on her heel and walk away.

But she stood her ground, it would have been asking for trouble to do anything else, and the smile that she switched on in answer to his was wide and brilliant and completely false.

CHAPTER TWO

'HELLO, Lucy, I'm glad you could come.' Daniel Stewart's voice was attractive enough to be an actor's, and hearing his voice she disliked him even more.

'Hello, Daniel,' she said. Now that it was too late she was realising that she should have had a good long talk with Celia before she'd tried to play the part of a girl who had had a holiday affair with this man. She hardly knew the first thing about him. She could show herself up as an impostor every time she opened her mouth.

That kept her mouth shut, the wide smile stretching it nervously like a clown's grin. Four more customers edged past them, through the archway into Falstaff Bar, calling across to friends, adding to the babel, and Daniel Stewart said, 'We're not going to hear ourselves speak in there, shall we go into the dining room?'

'I can't stop—I must get back. I just looked in to say hello, but I'm working on a rush job.' She hoped she was mistaken in hearing a rising note of panic in her own voice.

'Have you eaten?' he asked, and like a fool she admitted, 'No.'

'Then you should.'

The dining room was just across the foyer, and she went with him because she could hardly stand here and start arguing. Besides, if she just turned and ran that would solve nothing. She had to keep cool, so she sat in the chair he moved out for her, at a table for two by the window, and asked, 'What are you doing in my town? And don't say you came looking for me.'

She didn't sound provocative so much as grumpy. The last thing she wanted was to put herself across as attractive or amenable. Nor did she want him paying for her dinner, but she'd have to deal with that later.

'Taking a couple of weeks' holiday,' he said, and she was no wiser whether he had chosen this town because of Celia or not. It was tourist country, in the heart of England, lots of people did come holidaying here and there was plenty he could occupy himself with for fourteen days.

She wondered what he had planned for the nights, and if that was why he had contacted 'Lucy', and wished she could say, 'You're not my type, buster, never were.' But that would blow her cover wide. What she had to do was project a growing boredom, a holiday romance going sour. She had to leave him asking himself—whatever did I see in her? And, sitting opposite, he was looking at her with a conjecturing gaze.

His eyes were a piercing grey, and with daylight still streaming through the windows she wished they had been seated in one of the alcoves. This was altogether too much in the open when she was out to fool him.

Why didn't he say something? What was he checking for? He wasn't just a handsome face either. It was an intelligent face, the eyes were keen and the expression was reflective. This was a man who would be hard to trick, and it seemed to her that the silence was turning sinister and she floundered frantically for words that wouldn't sound forced or false.

'How are you keeping these days?' That was safe enough. You always asked people that.

'Very well, thank you.' But he continued to study her, sitting back in his chair, looking at her hair, face, hands, until she snapped.

'What's the matter with me? What are you staring at?'

'Sorry,' he said, but his smile was unrepentant and he didn't sound as if he was apologising. Lucy took a deep breath. If she blundered she'd have to pretend she'd forgotten. It had all happened twelve months ago.

For all he knew she could have had any number of affairs since then. He could be a long way down the list.

'Let's see,' she said, 'you're a photographer, aren't you?'

'That's right.' He didn't seem surprised that she wasn't sure, so he couldn't be very well known. What kind of photography? she wondered, and had a mental picture of him taking hundreds of shots of model girls, fashion pictures, that sort of thing, and getting some super studies because most of the girls would be fancying him, and come out all dewy-eyed and sexy-lipped.

'Had a good year,' she asked.

'Interesting,' he said. 'How about you?'

She shrugged, 'Oh, you know. Still painting my furniture.'

'I saw some of your work in the shop.' Now he sounded surprised, as though something hadn't fitted in with his expectations. 'You're very talented,' he added, and the compliment seemed sincere and she almost blushed.

'Thank you. Can I interest you in something expensive?' That might be a way to make sure he wouldn't come to the shop again, but he said.

'You might well,' and turned to take one of the menus that the waitress was offering. The girl beamed at him as though he was a favourite customer, and said confidentially,

'The duck's very good tonight.'

Lucy bobbed her head down behind the large cardboard folder. She would have liked to hold it up as a little shield for the rest of the meal. 'Do you remember the mézé?' Daniel asked her, and she just stopped herself saying, 'The what?'

Greek food, of course. Celia had enthused about it for a while after her holiday, but what was mézé? 'Mmm, yes,' Lucy said noncommittally. 'I think I will have the duck. It's Aylesbury duckling here, it's usually very good.'

It was better to be vague about their last meeting. If she was too pat, with the few details she had, he might think she'd been reliving them in her memory all these months. She was sure that Celia hadn't. Celia had almost forgotten Daniel Stewart, until Lucy phoned her this afternoon and told her that a man with that name was here.

He ordered the duck for both of them, and Lucy wondered how she was going to get through the meal. She *had* been reckless coming here, although she had only intended a quick drink in the bar, where the lights weren't so bright, and there was noise and people constantly eddying around.

Sitting in the dining room, in direct view and comparative quiet, facing what could turn into a third degree, was something else; and the palms of her hands were sweating. She could feel beads of perspiration breaking out on her top lip too, and she poured herself a glass from the jug of iced water and gulped a little.

Daniel Stewart consulted her on the wine list. She had been going to say, 'No, thank you,' but a glass of wine might take some of the tension out of her. She was a natural chatterer. She liked talking to people and getting them talking to her, but tonight she had to be careful. She mustn't say the wrong thing, she mustn't be too animated. Bored and boring, that was the idea, and this delicious food was going to be wasted on her.

She looked uneasily at the generous helping of duckling and all the side dishes. There was at least half an hour's eating time here and in half an hour he was surely going to realise that this was not the girl he had known in Cyprus. 'Where do you sell your photographs?' she asked perkily. He'd probably told Celia that. Well, she'd forgotten, hadn't she? That wouldn't do much for his ego, she bet most women remembered what he did.

'Newspapers,' he said. 'Magazines.'

She wrinkled her brow. 'You do take fashion photographs, don't you?'

'Sometimes,' he said. He could have been a model himself. He was wearing a lightweight suit, in dark grey, and a thin grey polo-neck sweater. With the right lighting, and the right setting, he would look a knockout. A Shelley, a Byron. Now that Lucy had seen him it was a little easier to understand how Celia had felt when they'd sat at adjoining tables, both alone, and the glass of wine had been knocked over and he had smiled across.

She drank deeply from her own glass of wine and said, 'I certainly never expected to see you again,' as though it was not an unmixed pleasure. As soon as the meal was finished she would insist on paying her share, and she would say, 'It's been nice seeing you again, I do hope you have a good holiday,' and if he said anything about another date she'd say, 'No, thank you,' and leave it at that.

They talked about the town for a few minutes; he'd spent the afternoon walking up to the ruins of a Cisterian abbey across the hills. Lucy recommended several other trips, getting her meal down as fast as she decently could because she was very anxious to get away.

Celia was a slow eater, Lucy was usually rushing off somewhere, but rarely with the urgency of tonight. Celia had taken meals with this man on holiday—at the hotel, probably while they were sightseeing together. Perhaps he was remembering that Celia never gobbled away like this, and Lucy said, 'I told you, I have to get back to work, I have this table to finish.'

It was a shame not to savour the food, but the longer she lingered the more likely she was to get acute indigestion. If she chewed every mouthful slowly, waiting for Daniel Stewart to say, 'You're not Lucy, who are you? What goes on?' she would be a nervous wreck before coffee came.

'Tell me about the table,' he said, and she seized on
that as a safe subject, describing the design, the colours.
It was almost finished and the customer, who had
looked in a couple of days ago to check on progress,
had said that his wife was going to be thrilled to
death with her birthday surprise. Lucy smiled now,
because satisfied customers were lovely.

'It sounds splendid,' said Daniel Stewart.

'I am rather pleased with it.'

She wished he wouldn't look at her, she wished she
hadn't come, she wished she could think of something
else to talk about. She said, desperately, 'I'm sorry, I
forget, do you have a family?'

If he had a wife and children that was going to be
a remarkable lapse of memory on her part. He could
be married. Celia hadn't said. Celia was married and
she hadn't let it stand in her way.

'No,' he said. He poured more wine for her, but she
had had enough, she wasn't drinking any more. 'You
have a sister, don't you?'

'Oh yes.' She couldn't look up at him. She chewed
on a sautéed potato, and poked around in the rata-
touille on her plate as though she was allergic to one of
the ingredients and had to remove all traces of it.

'Is she like you?' Had he asked Celia that? What
had Celia said? If there had been less at stake Lucy
would have given up here and now, and admitted she
was a fraud, but there was nothing lighthearted about
this situation, and she was responsible for the turn it
had taken.

She shouldn't have come here, kidding herself that
she could handle Daniel Stewart with a few well
chosen words. Celia was to blame for what had happened in Cyprus, but it was entirely Lucy's own fault
that she was here now, in the hot seat, being grilled by
a smiling man with piercing eyes.

The last thing she must do was squirm away from
his scrutiny. He'd know then for sure that she was

bothered about something. She must keep her wits about her and not say anything stupid. 'We're close,' she said, 'my sister and I, but we're not very alike. She has a husband and family and I'm more interested in my business than in settling down.'

'Yes, of course.' They ate for a few moments in silence, then he started to ask, 'Do you remember——' and she said briskly:

'Probably not.' Until she talked to Celia he could catch her out in a hundred ways. She said, 'I'm sorry, but I'm not much for memory lane. Come-day go-day, I always say.'

She didn't think she'd ever said come-day go-day in her life. How did it finish? 'God send Sunday.' God get me through the next half hour, she thought. I'll settle for that. She put down her knife and fork. 'That was super, but I really must go now.'

'The table,' he said.

'It has to be finished, you see.'

'Of course it does.' He stood when she did, and to her alarm pushed his chair up to the table.

'I mustn't take you from your meal,' she said, but he was signalling to the waitress, who came with a worried face asking,

'Wasn't it all right?'

'Delicious,' said Daniel Stewart, 'but we have to be getting along.'

'Oh dear!' She started writing out the bill for him to sign while Lucy was protesting,

'You don't need to come. I shall be working. I do wish you'd stay and finish your meal.'

He took no notice. He walked with her out of the dining room and across the foyer, and she waited until they were outside the hotel before she said any more. Then she said, 'It was nice meeting you again, but I think we should call it a day now.'

'Do you? Why?'

Aunt Dolly was right, he was tall. His hair flopped

a little in the night breeze and the beautifully chiselled mouth was curved in a half smile. The conceit of the man! Lucy thought; he imagines he can walk into a girl's life and carry on just where they left off. 'I would very much like to see some more of your work,' he said. 'Do you object to customers in the studio?'

'Well, no.' If she said the shop was shut he'd be along in the morning. There was no good reason why he shouldn't walk along now and look, if he genuinely wanted to buy, although she would have been a lot happier leaving him here.

'That's all right, then,' he said, and she moved because she didn't want him taking her hand or her arm. She wasn't going the length of the high street swinging hands with him, probably getting spotted by someone who knew her and who would want to know afterwards what was going on. If Daniel Stewart had been less striking it wouldn't have mattered, but she wasn't having women buttonholing her for the next few weeks and saying, 'I say, who was that I saw you holding hands with on Thursday night?' She could hardly tell them, 'A man who thought he slept with me in Cyprus. Only it wasn't me, it was Celia.'

'A business acquaintance,' she could say, so long as they remained detached, and she walked fast although she was jittery with nerves, wondering what she was going to do when they reached the shop if Aunt Dolly decided to come down and say hello.

She talked as she walked, partly from nerves and partly to stop him harking back to Cyprus. She pointed out the shops and houses they were passing, and told him who owned them and ran them, chattering like a magpie.

'You know your neighbours,' he said laconically, when she paused to draw breath.

'I've lived here all my life. Well, more or less. The shop's always been here although my home's in Avington, about three miles away. Here's our road down here, the shop's just down here.'

He'd been in the shop this afternoon, so he knew that. She couldn't go straight into the workshed because the workshed keys were in the cottage and her key opened the side door to the shop. She took him under the archway and was undecided whether to say, 'Stay here, I won't be a minute.' But having opened the front door it was easier to let him follow her in. He could look around the shop while she dashed into the cottage and did a little censored explaining.

She went through the connecting door, calling, 'It's only me!' and Aunt Dolly and Uncle Joe, watching television in the living room, turned smiling faces towards her.

'I've brought a friend back, he wants to see the dining table I'm doing,' said Lucy, and as Aunt Dolly craned to see round her into the hall she added, 'I left him in the shop.'

Aunt Dolly nodded meaningly at Uncle Joe, who had obviously been told all about the handsome caller and the dinner invitation. 'How long's he stopping for?' asked Aunt Dolly, and Lucy blinked.

'Stopping? He's not stopping. He's just come to look at the table. He thinks he might buy something.'

'I mean how long will he be at the Crown?'

'I don't know,' Lucy fibbed. She took the small ring of keys from the wooden bowl on the sideboard, where they were deposited each evening.

'He was the one you thought he was, then?' Aunt Dolly persisted. 'The one you met on holiday?'

'Er—yes,' said Lucy, and fled.

When she re-entered the shop Daniel was standing in front of a three-section screen that she had painted with a winding lane going over a hill. Fluffy clouds hung in a clear blue sky and hedgerows, bright with wild flowers, edged the lane. 'What's over the hill?' he asked her.

'Whatever you want.' She had amused herself, wondering that, while she was painting it. 'How about a village, full of people you like?'

'Or more open road, just winding on?' No, she thought, you wouldn't come quietly to a village. You'd be more likely to roar through in a sports car making for far horizons.

'Perhaps,' she said.

'I like it.'

'Ah, but would it go with your decor? What kind of home do you have?'

He laughed, 'You're right. It's a small furnished apartment and I'm not in it very much.' He turned from the screen. 'Tell me,' he said, 'did you get any inspiration from Cyprus?'

Her face burned and her heart jerked suddenly. He thought that he had lain with her in his arms, her naked flesh against his, and for the moment she felt as vulnerable as though they had been lovers. 'But of course,' she said quickly. 'Wherever I go I'm always looking for ideas. But I don't think I've got anything at the moment with a Cyprus theme.'

He was a man she had never set eyes on till today, who had never touched her, much less made love to her, and she had to get the conversation off Cyprus. She went on, 'You travel a lot in your job, I suppose. Could I interest you in a bow-topped vardo?'

She expected him to ask, 'What's that?' not 'Have you got one?'

'This way, sir,' and she led him out of the shop, round the back of the workshed into the garden behind the cottage. Aunt Dolly's vegetable and herb patch took up half the space, but there was a little lawn and, in the middle of the lawn, a gipsy waggon, with the old bow-top and shafts for the horse, and steps in place before the door.

Lucy had painted the woodwork in a riot of roses and castles, serpents and symbols, and Daniel Stewart stopped dead in his tracks to ask, 'Did you do this? It's bloody marvellous!'

She was proud of her vardo, flattered that he was so impressed, and she told him, 'We bought it a couple of years ago. It was a wreck, but Uncle Joe restored it and I painted it. Some of the designs are original, I followed them where you could see them, the rest I did in traditional style. I finished it just after Christmas.'

'You're never going to sell it?' He was walking around, peering close and then standing back and taking the far view, with an enthusiasm that had her smiling.

'No.'

'Of course you're not. You couldn't let this go.' And suddenly there seemed to be a rapport between them as though his arrogance and her antagonism were in abeyance for a while. For the first time she relaxed.

'I'm not selling it,' she assured him. 'I like it, it's mine. Besides, it's a sales gimmick. We take it to the village fairs. It catches the eye, it gets orders. People decide they'd like some gipsy roses on a kitchen dresser, and the snakes are a good seller too. Funny, that, isn't it?'

'I don't know.' He was looking at a purple and cerise serpent coiled on the top panel of the door. 'That might make unwelcome callers think twice. Can I go inside?'

Lucy climbed the steps and turned the key. Little curtains were drawn so that it was dark inside. Evening shadows were beginning to fall, but when she pulled back the curtains there was still light enough to see the furnishings: bunk, table, bench, cupboards, and a black stove behind the door.

The waggon was always a star attraction, and sometimes Lucy dressed up as a fortune-teller, and the takings went to whichever village church was holding the fête.

She sat at the table now while Daniel examined every piece of furniture, every painted motif, with a flattering absorption. She could imagine he would be fun to go sightseeing with, in Cyprus or anywhere else. He wouldn't miss much. If Celia had spent all her holiday till then sitting around the hotel no wonder she'd woken up when he'd taken over.

'Do you use it?' he asked Lucy. 'Hitch up and take off?'

She looked through the open door at the empty shafts. 'We hitch up a horse when we go to the fairs. His name's William, we borrow him from a farmer friend of ours, but I've never made for the open road.'

'Didn't you ever want to?' He came and sat beside her and she thought—you're a tempter and I wouldn't trust you an inch. But she said,

'Now you mention it I might at that, some time.'

'Shall we? How about a didikai?'

She laughed, 'I don't see you as a Romany Rye.'

'Part Romany?' She started to shake her head and he said,

'I spent three months with a family of Spanish gipsies once.'

'Doing what?'

'Travelling. Taking photographs.'

And then she could imagine him sitting by a campfire, at night when the flames threw dancing shadows, looking like a handsome gipsy; and the girls with dark tumbling hair, like a scene from *Carmen*. She said, 'I'll bet that was fun.'

Daniel smiled and said nothing and she got up. 'Well, you've seen the vardo. Now do you want to see the table?'

'Yes, please.' She didn't want to sit there beside him, in the shadowy little room of the caravan, any longer. She locked that door, and opened the workshed, then turned on the strip lighting so that he could see everything in here at a glance.

The pieces were in varying stages. The dining table was the nearest to completion and he looked at that first. 'Oh yes,' he said.

'Thank you. I have to get on with it now. I have to get it finished.'

She pulled the old paint smock over her head and, while he walked around the workshed, she touched one of the leaves that encircled the table's edge, with the darker paint that made the tracery of veins. Daniel moved quietly, but she was always aware of him, and after a few minutes she said 'I'm sorry but I can't paint while I'm being overlooked. If you've seen everything—'

'Of course,' he said. He had been standing close to her. She didn't usually mind who watched, but Daniel was managing to make her nervous. She put down palette and brush, and she knew he was going to kiss her and there wasn't much she could do about that.

She had been kissed before often enough, enjoying it sometimes more than others, but Daniel Stewart was an expert. His mouth took hers, warm and sensuous, and she felt a tingling shock of pleasure, as the kiss deepened, that could have triggered an instinctive response. Kissing him back would have been crazy, but she nearly did just that.

Instead she pulled away and he said, 'Goodnight. Lucy,' and walked out into the shadows of the yard while she was still gasping. That was altogether too intimate a kiss for a near stranger, but of course he thought they had been lovers. He must have kissed Celia that way, and other ways, and Lucy found that she was frantically rubbing her mouth with the back of her hand as though there was something on her lips that was scalding her.

He hadn't said 'Goodbye,' just 'Goodnight,' so she would probably be seeing him again, and she must have her plan of campaign clear in her mind before then. There was no margin here for emotional muzziness.

She was sleeping at the cottage tonight, it was up early in the morning, Saturday was market day, and she would have liked to go next door and sink into an easy chair for an hour or two before bedtime. But Aunt Dolly would have a barrage of questions ready, so Lucy stayed down in the workshed, working on the table, for the best part of another hour.

Then she started filling a large oval basket with some of the small items they were hoping to sell from their stall. They always took along a few pieces of furniture, usually including a dresser on which china and pots could be displayed. There were always painted window boxes and jewellery boxes, and an assortment of attractive not-too-pricey Victorian and Edwardian bygones.

Uncle Joe came down when the basket was almost filled, and looked surprised to find her alone in the stockroom. 'Your young man gone, then?' he enquired, and she went on tucking in newspaper.

'He is not my young man!'

'Dol seems very taken with him.' Uncle Joe dragged forward an empty packing case in which they transported some of the unbreakables, from old flatirons to brass candlesticks.

'He's a good-looking bloke,' Lucy admitted.

'That's all?'

She shrugged as though she was considering the question and finally decided, 'I should think so, yes.'

'Funny,' said Uncle Joe, placing an iron doorstopper in the shape of a black sheepdog at the bottom of the packing case, 'Dol's never been one for putting too much value on appearance.' He chuckled. 'Or she'd never have married me, would she?'

'Go on,' Lucy teased, 'you know you look like Gregory Peck.' Uncle Joe was over six foot tall and so was Mr Peck, but there the resemblance ended and both he and Lucy knew it. That was why they laughed together, and afterwards got on with the packing.

This was a regular Friday evening chore, getting the market stock together. The market filled the main road on Saturday and Uncle Joe went along around eight o'clock in the morning to set up the stall. Partridge and Friis had had the same position since before Lucy and Celia were born, one of the best sites, under the arches of the old medieval cheese market, in the middle of the town. The stone arches were open to the elements, but a roof gave some protection from wind and rain.

Lucy always enjoyed market days. Her fellow traders were a good-humoured colourful bunch, and kind; and she liked the thronging crowds, the chat and the bustle. She usually went to bed on Friday nights in happy anticipation of a good day tomorrow, and fell asleep easily. But tonight she was too worried to sleep, and half expecting Celia to phone her.

She often had her little radio on beside her bed, but tonight she was listening for the ringing of the phone bell down in the office. She tried to read, but it was hopeless, and she had turned out the light, and decided that Celia hadn't been able to get to a phone and that she must get to sleep, when the phone rang.

She was out of bed in a flash. It was a couple of minutes after eleven and Uncle Joe might be awake, or still pottering around. Lucy wanted to reach the phone first, and she didn't stop for slippers or dressing gown. She was out on the little landing, barefoot and in a white cotton nightshirt, calling, 'I'll get it!' as she passed Uncle Joe and Aunt Dolly's bedroom door.

There were no lights, so they must be in bed. She switched on a few, the final one in the shop, to prevent her bumping into anything in her rush towards the office and the ringing bell. It was cold down here, after her snug little bed. 'Hello?' she said. 'Celia?' and felt the chill air settle on her skin like a fine mist.

'What happened? Did you get through?' It was Celia, and Lucy asked,

'Can you talk?' before she started answering questions.

'I'm on my own. Howard's staying on, but I came away early. I was tired.' More worried than tired, Lucy suspected, and with good reason.

'I saw him,' she said. 'I went to the Crown,' and as Celia croaked, 'Oh my God!' she added, quickly and reassuringly, It's all right. He was waiting for Lucy Friis and I am Lucy.'

'Why ever did you do that?' Celia·screeched. 'What did you talk about?'

'There wasn't much about Cyprus, I can tell you. I only meant to walk in and chill him off, but I found myself with a meal in front of me. I got that down in about ten minutes flat, then I said I had to get back to work, and he came back here with me and he saw the vardo.'

'The what?'

'The gipsy waggon.' Celia knew all about the waggon, but she wasn't very interested in the shop, nor in what was sold there, although she quite liked Lucy's work. 'He was only here a few minutes,' said Lucy.

'Will he be back?'

'I don't know.' In the shop, through the open office door, Lucy could see the screen with the vanishing road, in front of which Daniel had stood. He was a traveller, always moving on, but he hadn't said good-bye tonight. She said, 'I surely hope not, because I wouldn't know what to say to him. I don't know what happened. Where you went sightseeing, that sort of thing.'

'I can't remember.' Celia sounded as if she was speaking with clenched teeth, rigidly holding back the memories, and Lucy said,

'All right, that's all right, I won't remember much,

but I've got to know something. You'll have to tell me a bit more than you've told me already. Can I come over tomorrow after the market?'

'How long is he staying?' Celia countered.

'Two weeks, he said. He's on holiday here.'

She heard Celia taking a deep breath, making a decision. 'I'm going up to London with Howard tomorrow, and I'm stopping there until Daniel's well away from Moreton Meadows.'

Howard had a service apartment near Westminster, where Celia sometimes stayed with him, taking the children and their nanny. This time she was running away, and it wasn't a bad idea, but Lucy had to see her first. 'Look, love,' Lucy pointed out, 'if he does catch on that I'm a phoney we're in trouble. I'll get rid of him for you, but you've got to brief me. If you won't have time tomorrow you'd better do it now.'

There was silence, then Celia whispered, 'I *can't*. I'm sitting here and Howard's photograph's looking at me.'

That meant she was downstairs in her warm little sitting room, still wearing her evening finery, and Lucy—in nothing but a cotton nightshirt, standing on flagstones, feeling chilly draughts eddying around her—said wearily, 'Then turn out the light or flatten the photograph.'

'I can't talk about it now,' Celia cried. 'And I think I can hear Rolly.'

The children both slept in the nursery. Their nurse had the connecting room and if Rolly was calling out Nanny would soon be in to attend to him. Celia wouldn't hear him downstairs in the small sitting room, unless he was yelling his head off. She was just making an excuse to hang up, and Lucy could understand her reluctance to talk about the time she had spent with Daniel Stewart. But she couldn't blot out the whole thing and run for London, leaving Lucy playing a part when she didn't even know the words.

'Don't you hang up. You listen to me,' Lucy said urgently. 'You've got to talk, but how about taping it?' They both had small radio-tape recorders. 'Chat up a tape and take it round home tomorrow and leave it in my dressing table drawer.'

'Suppose Maman found it?' Celia asked in breath-less horror.

'I've got my cassette player here, and she doesn't know one end of a tape from another,' Lucy pointed out, but Celia was still fearful.

'It would be like signing a confession. If you left it lying about——'

'I'm not that daft.' Lucy wanted to shake Celia, but she had to keep calm and anyhow she couldn't shake somebody who was several miles away. 'I'd wipe it clear. Of course I would.'

'You are scatty sometimes, though, aren't you?' Celia sounded as though she was coming up with a trump card, and Lucy was supposed to be the scatty sister, although she was the one earning a good living and running a profitable business. 'You can't realise just what this could mean to me,' moaned Celia. 'It isn't a joke. It isn't funny.'

Lucy was stung to the quick, because the last few hours had been painful and full of fear, and the fear had been for her sister. She said bitterly, 'I don't think it's funny, and I know darn well what could happen if Howard found out, and I think you were a stupid cow to take a chance like that.'

She had never spoken like this to Celia before, they had never quarrelled before in Lucy's recollection, and she could imagine Celia, stunned with surprise, the soft mouth falling open. 'I'm not suggesting you talk about sleeping with the man,' Lucy went savagely on. 'I can do without a graphic description of that. You don't need to mention him at all, just talk about where you went and what you ate, anybody you met, anything he's likely to come up with to catch me out.

And if I should be idiot enough to leave it lying around, and somebody should decide to play it, that would be all it was, a bit of holiday chat. Maybe I'm thinking of going to Cyprus and you're telling me what it's like.'

'I'm sorry,' said Celia, shaken and subdued. 'I've got a good hour before Howard's due home, I'll do a tape for you, and in the morning I'll go round and say goodbye to Maman and put it in your dressing table drawer.'

By now Lucy was half frozen and her teeth were chattering. 'You do that,' she said. 'Goodnight.'

'I know you want to help me,' Celia's voice came wailing through the receiver as Lucy took it from her ear, and she held the phone, looking at it, 'and I shouldn't have given your name, and I'm sorry.'

Lucy upended the mouthpiece to say, 'What's in a name? You don't have to apologise to me, it's Howard who's the injured party.' Then she put the phone on the cradle whether Celia had finished or not.

She wasn't herself tonight. She was really upset. She wished she could have taken off for London. Or for anywhere that would have kept her out of Moreton Meadows until Daniel Stewart had finished his holiday and gone on his way.

CHAPTER THREE

Lucy was wrapping up a small red glass dish when the shadow of Daniel Stewart fell across her. Well, that was how it seemed, because she sensed him before she saw him. Then she peered out of the corner of her eye, her hands still busy with the package, and there he was, smiling and saying, 'Hello.'

The woman who was buying the glass dish looked round and hoped he was smiling at her, and he was, at both of them; although the hello was for Lucy, who gave him a grudging, 'Hi,' in return.

Lucy was on her own, she usually did run the market stall single-handed until Aunt Dolly came along and relieved her at lunch time, shutting the shop for an hour. She was glad Uncle Joe had gone—once all was set up he went back to his workshed—and Aunt Dolly hadn't arrived when Daniel turned up.

He was looking as handsome as he did last night, and that meant that most women who passed him took a second glance, and Lucy felt irritation welling up in her again. 'What do you want?' she demanded.

'Not a thing,' he said. 'Just taking a stroll round the market.'

There was no law against that, but she wished he would move on now instead of lounging against the end of her stall, his eyes cool and mocking and missing nothing.

A girl, rooting through one of the jewellery trays, selected a brooch with a green stone, and Daniel said, 'It matches your eyes.' Her eyes weren't that green, but her eyeshadow was, and Lucy watched her go pink-cheeked with pleasure.

'I think I'll have it,' she said, and handed it across

to Lucy while Daniel continued to chat, asking was she on holiday? Yes, she said, she and her friend were here on a day trip.

'It's an interesting town, isn't it?' he said. 'And you're getting good weather.'

'Smashing,' said the girl, and she wasn't talking about town or weather.

'What kind of scissors are those?' a man with an American accent asked him, pointing to a small ornate pair of scissors with oddly shaped blades. Daniel went behind the stall to pick them up and examine them, then grinned,

'Damned if I know. Hey, darling, what were these used for?'

'They're Victorian grape scissors,' Lucy explained. 'To snip a few grapes off the bunch.'

'Not much call for that these days,' said Daniel. 'But if it's heirlooms you're after they're silver—here's the hallmark—and beautifully made.' He came round with them, and the man and his wife went into a little huddle, and considering he had just cheerfully admitted that he didn't know a pair of grape scissors when he saw them Daniel's spiel was a masterpiece.

He's a born salesman, Lucy thought. He'd get along on wits and charm anywhere. And he was enjoying himself. As soon as the grape scissors were wrapped up and carried away, he joined two women who were examining one of Lucy's painted stools.

'Handpainted, of course,' he informed them. 'And an original design.' They bought the stool, and took directions how to get to the shop and see the bigger items, and as they headed in that direction Lucy said drily,

'Maybe you should run on ahead and get there before they do. I don't think Aunt Dolly has quite your touch.'

'Your work sells itself, doesn't it?' he said, and she smiled at that.

'You think so? It does go fairly well, yes, but you're a salesman all right.' The silver grape scissors were one of the the priciest articles on the stall, and he'd sold them. Lucy was no mean salesgirl. Her pretty face and shining hair looked clean with a little-girl freshness, and her smile was quick and friendly. Folk tended to trust her on sight, to believe what she told them about the goods on her stall, and she wasn't out to cheat, so she had an earned reputation for fair dealing that brought the customers back again.

But Daniel wasn't waiting for the customers. He was catching them as they passed, often with just a smile and a word; and next thing they'd be discussing prints or brassware, or how inflation would have doubled the price of everything by this time next year, and often as not Lucy would find herself counting the change and wrapping up the purchase.

He had a novelty value with the locals, who knew Lucy and her stall. Ma Morris and Mavis her daughter, from home-made sweets and candies on the next site, never stopped staring, and Mavis was soon asking, 'Who is he?'

'A friend,' said Lucy, conducting a quick exchange of names.

'We can do with a few more like you around, Daniel,' said Mavis, chuckling until her three chins wobbled. 'Brightens the market up, doesn't he?' She nudged Lucy, nearly knocking her sidewards. 'I bet you didn't get him with a packet of tea!'

Daniel laughed too, quite naturally, as though he was amused at the joke, not laughing at Mavis, who went back, still chuckling, to go on weighing up quarter-pound bags of Morris's Gold-Medal Cotswold Cream Fudge.

'Most of the stallholders will know all about Daniel Stewart within the next half hour,' Lucy muttered, and Daniel shrugged.

'Not all,' he said, 'only the name.' Suddenly his eyes

looked straight down into hers. 'And a name doesn't tell you much, does it? Even if it is the genuine article.'

Her name was genuine, she was Lucy Friis. But Celia had given him a name that didn't belong to her, and Lucy was involved in that deception, and the market noises seemed to roar in her ears so that she almost had to shout, 'What do you mean?'

If he knew, he wasn't playing cat and mouse with her. But his smile was slow and easy. 'Well, if it's your real name that was your family and what the family chose for you. But if you decide to rename yourself, a pen-name, a stage-name, then it's probably more revealing.'

She said, 'I suppose so. But you haven't changed your name, you've always been Daniel Stewart?'

'Always. And you've always been Lucy.' She didn't think that was a question, she hoped it wasn't. She said,

'That's me.' All this talk about names was making her nervous and she prattled on, 'It's a dull name, I always feel. There was that dreary poem Wordsworth wrote, something about "few would know when Lucy ceased to be".' She grimaced. 'That kind of thing doesn't do much for your ego.'

He laughed. 'You don't look to me as though you'll be ceasing to be for a long time yet,' and she said abruptly.

'My sister's called Celia.'

'Is she?'

'She's very attractive.'

'I'm sure she is.'

'She's away on holiday now, but if you're still here when she and her family come back you must meet her.'

'Yes, I'd like that.' He sounded natural and casual, expressing an interest in an unknown woman out of common courtesy, and Lucy breathed freely again.

As Mavis had just said, Daniel certainly brightened

up the stall. Almost too good-looking to be true—even Lucy's regular customers were getting him to serve them; and as he was standing at the front of the stall, and Lucy was sitting on her stool behind the counter, he caught the eye first.

'I'm not paying you, you know,' she said, after a small flurry of sales, and knew she was being ungrateful.

'Tell you what.' He reached over the counter and caught her hand, 'I'll work for free for old times' sake.' She felt her breath come in a shuddering sigh, as she slid her fingers from his hold and said lightly,

'That's the kind of help I like.'

There was no denying it, he made market day even livelier than usual. He got people buying and he got Lucy laughing. He played a dozen parts, matching his approach to the customer, matey with the ones who were cheerful, turning on an aristocratic hauteur with well-corseted matrons and florid-faced gentlemen who considered themselves a cut above a stallholder.

'Let me see that, girl,' one woman ordered Lucy, pointing to a picture of a horse, and when Lucy brought it to her she sniffed. 'It's a print,' she glared at Lucy, who said,

'Sorry, but yes, it is. Most of them are.'

'I wouldn't hang a print on my walls,' the woman shuddered at the very thought, until Daniel drawled, with scornfully curled lip,

'And what were you expecting for two-fifty, madam? A Stubbs original?'

Aunt Dolly turned up at lunchtime, making a show of surprise at finding him here, although Lucy was sure she had known. There were at least half a dozen stalls where Aunt Dolly stopped to have a few words on her way along the high street to the Cheese Market. Someone would have told her Lucy had a very attractive young man helping out. But Aunt Dolly said,

'Well, hello, fancy you being here. Come to take Lucy to lunch, have you?'

'He's been here all morning,' said Lucy as she fished under the stall and came up with her handbag. 'And we've been busy too—I'm parched! You'll be okay now, will you?'

'Of course I will.'

Lucy usually wasted no time when Aunt Dolly arrived, but today she was so anxious to get Daniel away before Aunt Dolly started asking questions that she fairly zipped out from behind the stall, and cut through the crowds out of the Cheese Market into the road. Daniel kept pace with her, enquiring, 'Where do you usually eat?'

The Wheatsheaf, an old inn just down one of the side streets, was a kind of Saturday club for the market folk. Lucy usually had sandwiches and either coffee or a lager there, and met her fellow traders and swapped stories and gossip. Today she hoped there would be safety in numbers. Until she knew more about that Cyprus holiday she dared not sit talking with Daniel. She had to take him where the crowds were, and the bar was crowded as usual.

A space was found for Lucy on the end of a bench, as the sitters greeted her and moved up. Daniel went to the counter, to get a couple of ploughman's lunches and two lagers, and Lucy explained, 'He's a friend, a freelance photographer, he's helping me on the stall today.'

She was on tenterhooks that somebody might ask something awkward, like, 'Where did you find him?' If they did she would either say, 'On holiday last year,' and start talking about something else, fast; or smile sweetly and say, 'It was a pick-up.'

But she got through her lunch hour, and back at the stall Aunt Dolly said goodbye and then asked Daniel if he'd like to come to supper.

'Oh no!' gasped Lucy. 'I mean, I've got a date tonight.'

'I wasn't asking you,' Aunt Dolly twinkled. 'If Daniel can stand the company of two old folk.'

He could have pleaded a prior engagement, but instead he said he would be delighted to come to supper, and Lucy couldn't let it happen. Aunt Dolly would feed him royally, and within five minutes of letting him in through the front door she would know that he had met Lucy in Cyprus and Lucy had never been to Cyprus. But Celia had.

'Half past seven, then,' said Aunt Dolly, 'and Lucy, I'm sure your date isn't that important. Put them off— why don't you?'

In fact Lucy had a free evening ahead, but even if she had had a fantastic outing planned she would have had to cancel, because she had to be there when Aunt Dolly started probing. Aunt Dolly was a menace, she was going to blow the whole thing, out of sheer loving concern for Lucy.

Seeing Daniel, helping at the stall, she had decided that Lucy had to like him and it would be nice to ask him along to supper. It was ironic that Aunt Dolly was so impressed by a man who was a great deal more likely to bring Lucy tragedy than happiness.

For a moment Lucy considered telling the Partridges what the real situation was, but Aunt Dolly would have been shocked rigid at the idea of Celia, with her lovely children and her loving husband, carrying on like that. If Lucy, for all her youth and tolerance, couldn't understand it herself, how could she expect Aunt Dolly to? And the next time Maman proudly produced a photograph, or said something about how absolutely splendid Celia was, Aunt Dolly's disapproving expression would be a complete give-away.

Maybe I'll pick a row with him tonight, Lucy thought. Anyhow, I'll tell him I don't want to see him again. She asked, 'Are you going to hang around here all afternoon?'

'I'm enjoying myself,' he said.

'Funny way to spend a holiday.'

'It's not Cyprus, I grant you. Except,' he grinned so wickedly that she couldn't meet his eyes, 'that we're together.'

'It's different from Cyprus in every way,' she snapped, and turned to a girl who was looking thoughtfully at the price label on a jug and offered to knock off twenty-five pence.

At closing down time Daniel still seemed full of energy, but Lucy was tired and dusty. Uncle Joe had arrived to help with packing and loading the unsold stock, and Daniel helped to dismantle the stall. Lucy couldn't imagine Uncle Joe quizzing Daniel, but she would have been uneasy about leaving them alone. She often did leave Uncle Joe to finish off, and walked back to the shop herself, but tonight she had to stay until the last packing case was lifted into the van, and when she said goodbye to Daniel he said, 'I'd like to see you tonight.'

'You might.' She bit her lip. 'I might be there.'

He thought she was cancelling her date. He smiled and she thought—Don't kid yourself, I'm not standing anybody up because you've materialised after twelve months.

Of course he was conceited, he was too good-looking to be anything else. This was what he expected, that when he chose to walk back into a girl's life—even if it was only for a few days and then he'd be away again—she would fall palpitating into his arms.

As Lucy and Uncle Joe started to unload in the yard of the shop she said, 'Aunt Dolly's asked him to supper.'

Uncle Joe grunted, meaning he knew that, and between them they carried the big oval basket into the storeroom. 'I wish she wouldn't,' Lucy muttered.

'Why not?' They set down the basket and she said,

'Because—he could be married for all I know, he could be anything.' Her face was flushed and she was practically wringing her hands. 'I hardly know a thing about him. I met him ages ago and he's just decided to look me up again, and I don't trust him all that much.' Uncle Joe said nothing, and after a moment she gabbled on, 'He's too good-looking. He's too much of a good thing altogether.'

She was sounding prejudiced to the point of silliness, and she knew that Uncle Joe was wondering what was behind this tirade. 'He's so conceited,' she burst out. 'I can't stand men who think they're so almighty marvellous!'

Now Uncle Joe was probably wondering if Lucy had been hurt the last time she'd met Daniel because she didn't usually take violent unreasonable dislikes. He said quietly. 'Then why don't you tell him you want nothing more to do with him?'

'I was going to, but he just came along and started helping on the stall, and Mavis and Ma Morris were all eyes and ears. And I had a busy day. I didn't get a chance.'

She had had a chance when they went for lunch, and of course there had been times during the day when she could have insisted that Daniel clear off. Uncle Joe thought she didn't know her own mind, he didn't realise the complexity of this set-up. 'I am going to tell him,' she insisted. 'I just don't want Aunt Dolly encouraging him.' She managed a faint smile. 'Once he tastes her cooking he could move in here for the rest of the holiday.'

Uncle Joe was glad Lucy was joking again. He told her she was looking tired, and he could manage the rest of the unloading if she wanted to get along home. 'See you later?' he said. She nodded and he smiled. She was coming to supper. She had spent all day with this young man, and now she was coming back to have supper with him. That didn't sound as though she couldn't stand him ...

Maman was in the drawing room with a couple of friends. Saturday night was her bridge evening. it had been for years. There were a dozen of them in the bridge club and tonight they were meeting at Lucy's home. The two friends had been helping Maman to cut the sandwiches and spread the rolls, and now the three ladies were taking a quiet cup of tea and discussing last week's game and tonight's tactics.

Lucy looked in, smiling at the two neighbours in their smart little suits, with their hair freshly washed and waved. 'Hello, you all look very cosy.'

Lucy liked the bridge ladies, she had known most of them all her life, and Maman was queen bee of that little coterie. But they all loved a gossip, and if the story of Celia's lapse ever got out it was possible that Maman would never enjoy playing bridge again.

Lucy was different. Lucy was the girl who came in looking grubby from a day behind a market stall, or hunting for second-hand furniture bargains. Lucy was more like their own sons and daughters, but Celia was the perfect one, and now Maman greeted Lucy with the news,

'Celia looked in this morning. She's gone up to London for a few days. Howard wanted her to go with him.' She smiled smugly. 'You know how he is, he can't bear to let her out of his sight. Really, they could still be on honeymoon.'

Lucy followed her mother's eyes to a family group photograph hanging on the wall, and said flippantly, 'Not with two children, surely!'

'These days,' sighed one of the bridge ladies, 'the honeymoon usually seems to come after the children.'

But not in their young days and never for Celia. Lucy said, 'Excuse me, I need to freshen up.'

'Will you be in this evening?' Maman asked.

'No, I'm going back.'

Maman's smile was sweet but vague. Lucy had a date, of course. She was a pretty girl, she had lots of dates and Maman liked to hear about them, but they couldn't compare with Celia's life-style. Celia was in London now, in the elegant little flat, mixing with people whose names were household words.

It was one of the bridge ladies who asked Lucy if she had had a good day. 'Lovely,' said Lucy. 'We did a roaring trade.' Maman never mentioned the market stall, although that and the shop—and Lucy's talents— were her livelihood as well as Lucy's. She would have preferred Lucy to do her painting on canvas instead of wood, it would have sounded more refined and less workmanlike.

The tape was under a top layer of scarves in Lucy's dressing table drawer. She found it as soon as she started looking and she left it on the dressing table, beside her cassette player, while she showered. Then she came back into her bedroom, and switched on the tape as she began to get dressed.

'Lucy?' Celia sounded as though she was making a phone call, and checking that it was Lucy who was listening. She cleared her throat and started again. 'Curium. You'd like Curium. I went there on my last day with some——' there was the faintest hesitation, 'some people from the hotel. It's an old town,' and she described the baths, the Roman theatre, the orange and lemon and grapefruit groves.

All the time Lucy kept thinking what a wonderful time Celia and Daniel must have had. Not the Celia she knew, a wilder, freer girl, laughing, throwing back her hair. This was the kind of descriptive stuff that could have come from a travel brochure, but occasionally Celia's voice changed, softened. 'There was a fantastic sunset and we sat watching it——' and Lucy could imagine the sunset, and the two in dark silhouette against the flaming curtain of the sky.

Celia was remembering while she was talking. 'That

night we had something called mézé,' she said, 'at this little café. There must have been about thirty separate dishes: salad, spinach in bacon rolls, whole sardines, chicken, squid.' She went on reciting them with an undertone of laughter in her voice, and Lucy guessed that the meal had been hilarious. Celia didn't do much giggling, but she sounded as though she had that day, eating mézé. So perhaps that was why Daniel had asked Lucy, 'Do you remember the mézé?'

That day Celia and Daniel had been lovers, and maybe the night before, and Lucy was wishing more strongly every minute that she hadn't been dragged into this. If Celia had had to break out and grab a piece of the permissive action, thought Lucy with a flash of unaccustomed cynicism, why hadn't she had the sense to cover her tracks? Why leave a trail heading straight back to Lucy?

Lucy had been dressing while she listened, and now she sat at the dressing table in a green spotted cotton skirt, the matching blouse on the bed, and dabbed moisture cream blobs on cheeks, chin and forehead, working the cream in slowly while Celia's revealing travelogue drew to a close.

'It's a beautiful country,' said Celia brightly. 'You'd love it, Lucy, you really must try for a holiday there. Maybe I'll come with you, I could show you around, couldn't I?'

'Thank *you*,' said Lucy

The tape turned in silence for a few seconds, and Lucy was just about to switch it back to review, and then wipe it clear, when suddenly Celia wailed, 'Oh, Lucy!' followed by a long quivering sigh, and Lucy froze.

'I'm so sorry.' All the false brightness had gone and Celia sounded on the verge of tears. 'And I'm sorry I said that you didn't understand and you might leave this tape lying around—I know you won't. I know you'll wipe it straight away, and Lucy, do be careful.

Please, *please* be careful for yourself, because he's *dangerous*.

'Talking like this has brought it all back. I'd tried to forget and I had forgotten, but I never thought he'd turn up again—and, Lucy, it wasn't my fault. It would have been all the same if he'd known I was married, a little thing like that won't bother Daniel for a minute. You know what they say about charming a duck off water—well, he can, and nothing's serious to him.

'He made a dead set for me and he's not fit to clean Howard's boots and I knew that, but—well, I'm an experienced woman, I got married at seventeen didn't I? And I've got a wonderful relationship with Howard. Everything, sex, everything, it's really good, we're really very well adjusted, but I've never been seduced before.'

She gave a bitter little laugh. 'That's what Maman would call him—a seducer. And I don't know what Maman would call me. She'd never forgive me, it would really wreck things for her. But this one is a seducer, and he's had it so easy—women, life, everything. He told me he'd never met a girl he couldn't get within twenty-four hours.

'He's completely selfish. No consideration for anyone else, no real feelings. But he's sexy and gorgeous to look at, and he's fantastic company, in and out of bed, and I'm scared to death that you might fall for him.

'You wouldn't stand a chance if he decided he wanted you, he'd sweep you off your feet, so you mustn't see him again. And not only because he might find out I gave him your name, but because he'd cause you a lot of pain and his sort aren't worth it, and I'd feel it was my fault, so keep right away from him, please. And Lucy, please wipe this right away.'

There was no more after that headlong rush of words, but Celia had said enough to destroy her life. This was evidence of adultery, a spoken confession, and

Lucy was touched at the concern that had made her sister take such a risk. She pressed a button and sat listening to the soft swish of the rewinding tape.

'He won't seduce me,' she said.

This was a Celia she had never suspected existed. For two days, in twenty-two years, Celia had played around, run wild; and Lucy, who had believed she knew her sister through and through, had been pole-axed with astonishment. But perhaps nobody knew anybody as well as they thought they did, because Celia was mistaken about Lucy. Nobody swept Lucy off her feet. She was a canny girl for all her impulsiveness.

Celia, married at seventeen, wasn't experienced. She was sheltered, protected. On her own she had been a gullible victim for an experienced womaniser. But Lucy had been fending off men who fancied their chances for years. She had always had to look after herself, and she knew most of the tricks of the game. Daniel Stewart's surface charm and staggering good looks would do him no good, because Lucy wasn't turned on by very handsome men who thought every girl in sight was crazy for them.

She pressed down the record button and let the tape run, recording nothing but wiping out Celia's indiscretions, while she continued to apply her make-up. She made up slowly, highlighting her cheekbones with a touch of silver shine, smudging eye-shadow with a fingertip. She and Celia had the same features, the same skin texture, but they used different brands of make-up. Celia stayed with the name she had used ever since she married—she hadn't been able to afford it before—while Lucy chopped and changed, trying out the new ideas in the reasonably priced ranges.

So they rarely even looked alike, and as she sat at the mirror, fixing her face, Lucy pondered on the contrast in their lives and characters. The joke was on

Daniel Stewart, imagining he was still dealing with the girl he had met in Cyprus. Lucy and Celia were twins, but they were not sisters under the skin. Under the skin they were two diametrically dissimilar women.

There was no danger that Lucy would be added to Daniel's score, fascinated by his frankly sensual appeal. Lucy could keep him at arm's length, and would; and somehow she would handle this affair so that he presented no future threat. When he left Moreton Meadows he must go determined that never, so long as he lived, would he be calling on Lucy Friis again.

He was an enemy who had to be scotched, and Lucy's expression was grave as she set her wits to the problem: how to do it, how to fix him. Vanity was probably his Achilles' heel. He would be expecting Celia-Lucy to be easy prey again, and that could be his big mistake, because this time he was up against a much less amenable girl.

She would warn him she was different from the girl he had met in Cyprus. He wouldn't know she meant that literally, and a small smile began to curve her freshly glossed lips. 'Nothing's the same here, on my home ground,' she would say. 'I feel we're almost strangers, although of course it's very nice to see you again.'

She would play him along, and block every serious move he made. She didn't approve of teases, but it was high time Daniel Stewart met one and got his come-uppance. After Lucy was through he would never again be able to claim that no girl could resist him, without knowing that he was lying.

It might improve him, deflate his ego, but of course he wouldn't thank her for that. He would dislike her heartily, which was just what was needed. She liked the plan. It seemed simple and sure.

She wasn't worried it might get out of hand, because she was confident that he was not a violent man. He was too smart to lose his head and make a complete fool of himself. In the end she'd get that look of arrogant disdain, and a drawling goodbye. He'd manage to convey that she was the loser, turning prude on him, that he couldn't care less. But for all that she was sure her rejection would be a body blow to his pride, and he wouldn't come back for more.

She looked good, slim and glowing, and tonight she was going all out to attract Daniel. The more he fancied her the sharper the shock when it was finally made clear that he wasn't getting her. She looked in again on Maman and her friends, and kissed Maman goodbye.

They all said how pretty she looked, and Maman agreed that the cotton separates were very nice, although she couldn't resist describing what Celia had been wearing this morning. A new expensive dress, with an Italian name.

'Who's the young man?' asked Alice Dyson, one of the bridge ladies, and Lucy said,

'Somebody I met a while ago. He's holidaying round here.' Then she went, before any more questions were asked.

Her luck ran out a mile out of the village, when the van stopped and she realised incredulously that the tank was empty. She had meant to fill it earlier, but with so much on her mind she had passed the garage coming home. It would be shut now, and although the owner lived in an adjoining bungalow there might be no one in, or they might not be answering the door.

Walking to town was out, cow parsley and grasses grew high on the verges and she was wearing high-heeled strap sandals, but this was a fairly busy road, plenty of cars passing at this time, and someone would give her a lift.

She stood by her car and started thumbing, and a little Mini driven by a large lady drew up. 'Having trouble, dear?' asked the lady, winding down the window.

'I'm out of gas. Could you get me to a garage, please?'

Things went smoothly after that. The garage owner's wife answered the door and, because Lucy was a regular customer, unlocked a pump and loaned her a can, and the Mini driver took her back to where her car was parked beside the road.

But it all took time. It meant that Lucy arrived at the cottage half an hour later than she had intended and in rather a flap. In thirty minutes Aunt Dolly would have had ample opportunity to question Daniel, and Lucy would have to say, 'Of course I've been to Cyprus—you're getting muddled, love.'

Later she would be forced to betray Celia's confidence to Aunt Dolly and Uncle Joe, because the main thing was keeping Daniel in the dark. Although he might well start wondering. She'd hate to have to appeal to him to say, 'Please go away. You were fooled out there, and I've been fooling you all over again. But you mustn't embarrass Celia, you see, because she moves in very superior circles and she was slightly out of her mind when she let you pick her up.'

The trouble was she could swear he had a streak of the devil in him. She didn't think he would meekly pack and leave. She felt it much more likely that he would go looking for Celia, if it was only for a joke, to extract a little malicious humour from the situation. And Celia was not equal to an encounter. She would fall apart. She had made a good job of pretending it had never happened, but now she had been forced to recall so much she was racked with conscience and terror. If Daniel Stewart phoned, or walked in, Celia would be telling all, and her happy home life, her 'wonderful relationship' with Howard, would come tumbling down like a tower of cards.

Lucy parked the van just inside the yard under the archway, let herself into the shop by the side door, and hurried through into the cottage. Once in the hall she made herself slow down. A few seconds weren't going to make much difference, and she didn't want to arrive breathless, she might have to do some quick talking.

Supper was usually eaten in the kitchen, but tonight, with a visitor, they were probably in the dining room. She opened the dining room door and there they were, the three of them around the table with a place laid for her. They were eating and Aunt Dolly gave a glad little cry. 'Ah—you came, we'd almost given you up. Oh, I am glad you came!' She was bustling to her feet. 'Sit you down, I'll get your plate. We've been having a very interesting talk and it's left us in a bit of a quandary. Now you can settle it for us.'

'Oh?' said Lucy.

This was it. She would have to brazen it out and perhaps Uncle Joe might catch on, but when Lucy insisted she had holidayed this time last year in Cyprus Aunt Dolly could well start producing postcards Lucy had sent her from Brighton.

Aunt Dolly went off to the kitchen and Lucy sat down and looked at the two men. Uncle Joe chewed on his mouthful of food, and Daniel smiled at her, with a flash of white teeth and a glint of dark grey eyes.

'This is delicious,' he said.

'Of course it is. She can turn a boiled egg into a banquet.' She could hear Aunt Dolly coming back. 'Well,' she said, squaring her shoulders and holding his gaze, 'what's this quandary, then?'

'I want to hire the waggon,' said Daniel, and Lucy almost choked.

'It's never been for hire.' Uncle Joe pointed out, and it was worth a lot of money and practically irreplaceable, but Lucy was so relieved that she found she was grinning broadly, asking,

'Where do you think you could get in the waggon?' You'd cause a traffic jam if you reached a town!'

Aunt Dolly put down a plate of honey-baked ham with trimmings and Lucy said, 'Looks super,' and picked up her knife and fork, while Daniel said,

'I'd skirt the towns. I'd like to start tomorrow morning, come back Tuesday night, and keep to the lanes, just wander round the Cotswolds.'

'Hitch up and take off?' she quoted what he had said to her. 'Could you handle the horse? Could we get the horse?'

But they had already phoned and checked that William was available, and Daniel explained that he had driven a waggon when he was living with gipsies in Spain. Uncle Joe mentioned the hiring price offered, which was good, and that he and Dolly had decided to leave it to Lucy.

Lucy knew at once that she wanted to say yes, because the waggon was only standing on that little patch of lawn, except for the rare occasions when they took it to the fairs. It ought to be rolling along the lanes. It had been a Romany living waggon, now it was just a museum piece. And Daniel had been enchanted with it. He would take good care of it.

She said slowly, 'I don't see why not.' She was still holding her knife and fork, but she hadn't started eating. 'Do you know round here?' she asked.

'Not very well.'

'We could map you out a route.' As though this was a real expedition instead of a slow amble within a ten-mile radius. 'I could come over one evening,' she offered, 'and have a meal with you.'

That would fit in very well with her plans. She could be seductive by moonlight, and it would be fun. They could light a small fire and play at being gipsies. She was beginning to feel as excited as a child.

Aunt Dolly gave Uncle Joe a look that said, 'I told you', and Lucy guessed that Uncle Joe had warned her that Lucy didn't want this affair rushed. Maybe he'd stopped her asking Daniel questions. But now Lucy was showing that if Daniel went off for a couple of days she was prepared to put herself out to join him for an hour or two.

'Why don't you come with me?' asked Daniel, and Lucy said,

'Mmm,' eyes sparkling, 'that would be great, but——' she sighed, 'I've got this table to finish, for one thing. I promised to have it ready by Tuesday. Although I suppose I could finish it tonight if I work late.'

If anybody was taking her vardo on to the open road she should be the one, and the temptation to say yes was strong. She looked at Aunt Dolly, who had the pucker of concern around her lips that she would have had if Lucy had suggested sharing her bedroom with Daniel, and smiled reassuringly, 'It's all right, love, there are separate bunks. Whole families used to sleep in them.'

'I could always pitch a tent outside,' Daniel suggested gravely, but of course he had no intention of doing that. He thought they would be carrying on from Cyprus, and one bunk would be all that was needed, so he had a surprise coming.

'I'll think about it,' said Lucy. 'But I will finish painting the table tonight.' She began to eat her meal, but she had already made up her mind that she was off with Daniel in the morning.

Uncle Joe produced a local map and worked out a route that would keep to the lanes and the smaller villages, not overtax William, and end each day in a good place to stay the night.

'The Dancing Stones,' Lucy frowned, looking down over his shoulder, to where a bony forefinger pointed, and he said,

'It's not too far and it's on Rollins' land and Daniel ought to see them. They're very historical.'

'Mmm,' said Lucy.

'Right. That's it, then,' said Uncle Joe, and he went down to the office phone to get permission to park

the waggon overnight; although there was no likeli-
hood of being refused as the land he had selected belonged to two farming cronies of his.

'We're playing it soft and safe, aren't we?' said
Daniel. 'Don't gipsies usually just draw up along the
hedgerows?'

'I don't know about you,' said Lucy, 'but I don't
fancy getting moved on at three o'clock in the morning.' Then she looked away because Daniel grinned,
agreeing that, 'Company at three in the morning
might be embarrassing.'

'I'd better get some bedding down there,' said Aunt
Dolly suddenly. 'And some food,' she added, but pre-
paring two bunks with as much space between them
as possible was top of Aunt Dolly's list, and when
Lucy looked in the waggon on her way to the workshed, the first thing she saw was the curtain.

There was a curtain rail near the ceiling, so that
the far end of the waggon could be divided from the
main area. There had never been a curtain up since
the waggon came here, but there was one now, with
small brass rings through the rail. It was in heavy dark
green moquette, and Lucy recognised it because it
usually hung behind the parlour door, a protection
from draughts. As this was summer there weren't many
draughts and Aunt Lucy seemed to think Lucy's need
was greater.

Lucy had walked ahead of Daniel, up the steps, and
she nearly fell backwards shaking with suppressed
mirth. 'What is it?' asked Daniel.

'My sleeping quarters,' said Lucy. A curtain wouldn't
keep anybody out, but obviously Aunt Dolly hoped
it might preserve the proprieties.

Daniel swished it aside. A pile of bedclothes lay
on the bunk behind it; sheets, pillows, blankets. Aunt
Dolly had chests and drawers full of linen, all smelling
of lavender. The sweet scent was filling the waggon and

Lucy said, 'My sleeping quarters, *if* I decide to come.'

He knew she would come. He thought they had been lovers and that tomorrow night they would be together, lying between these lavender-scented sheets. He didn't know that, far from being eager to make love with him, she was planning to make this trip the biggest let-down of his life.

But when his arms came tightly around her and he pulled her close, she rested against him for a moment, supple and pliable, smiling up as he smiled down. Then she said sweetly, 'You'd better not try seducing me while Aunt Dolly's still pottering around.'

'I wouldn't dream of it.' He held her a few seconds longer, sliding his hands down her slim body with a quick light touch, and there was something exciting in the brush of his fingers, like the tingle of a faint electric shock. Then he let her go and she said, 'And if I don't finish the table there'll be no chance of me getting away.'

He went into the workshed with her. She had told him she couldn't work easily when she was being watched, but either he had forgotten that or decided to ignore it. Anyhow, it wasn't true, she had said it to get rid of him, but if he wasn't down here tonight he would be in the cottage with Aunt Dolly and this was the lesser evil.

So she worked and he watched, and it needed extra concentration to keep her mind on the delicate tracery of leaves. She had expected him to talk, a flow of conversation would have been an added distraction, but he didn't. He sat down in an old wooden armchair and said nothing.

When she looked across he was watching her, and she explained, 'It has to have several coats of varnish on it when the design's finished, but Uncle Joe will do that for me.'

He nodded, and Lucy went on with the next leaf.

After a while the complete silence became a little un-
nerving, and she switched on Uncle Joe's old radio
so that music and voices made a background. She
painted carefully, absorbed in her task, but always
aware of the man just out of her range of vision unless
she turned her head to look at him. Once she started
asking how he had got into photography, when he had
decided that was what he wanted to do, and he said
briefly, 'It was a hobby. It still is.'

She believed him. He looked as though he would
earn his living in a way he found amusing and enter-
taining rather than in something that called for slog
or dedication. When he said no more she looked at
him, waiting, and he said, 'Get on with it, I want you
to finish this, I want you coming with me tomorrow.'

After that the only disturbance was Aunt Dolly, with
a tray of cheese and tomato sandwiches and two mugs
of cocoa; because Lucy hadn't finished her dinner,
hurrying down here to start painting the table.

'You've definitely decided, then?' said Aunt Dolly.
Daniel had jumped up to take the tray from her. Nice
old-fashioned manners my foot! thought Lucy. It's
all part of his stock in trade, spreading the charm
around.

'I'm going, yes,' she said. 'Thank you for fixing
things in the van and lending me the curtain.'

Aunt Dolly coloured slightly, said, 'It might get
cold at nights,' blushed deeper and hurried on, 'I've
put some tins and stuff in the food compartment and
I'll pack you a hamper for tomorrow.'

They were only off for a couple of days, passing
village stores where they could get everything they
needed, but if Aunt Dolly wanted to turn it into a
glorified picnic that was kind of her. Lucy wondered
if it would dawn on her eventually that, by cutting out
the need to shop or cook, she was providing them with
more time for what she would describe as 'larking
about.' Never, ever, as sex.

'Ah well,' sighed Aunt Dolly, 'I suppose I'm old-fashioned,' and to Lucy's protests that of course she wasn't she went, still looking worried, but resigned.

Daniel said drily, 'Should I have reassured her that my intentions are honourable?' He put down the tray on a workbench and offered the plate of sandwiches to Lucy, who took one and bit into it.

'Are they now?' Her voice was slightly muffled.

Honourable intentions used to mean being willing to marry the girl. Just that. Nothing to do with love or happiness. As she straightened she flexed her shoulders—she had been crouched over that table for well over an hour, and she felt stiff and tense. 'And what's an honourable intention these days?' she asked.

'Straightforward dealing? No deceptions?' He sat on the edge of the workbench, arms folded, long legs crossed at the ankles, watching her, and a pulse began to throb in her throat, catching her breath.

His intentions were straightforward enough. He wanted to take her as soon as possible. There was no hypocrisy here, he was stripping her with his eyes, caressing her with a look. She felt he could almost possess her without touching, the little space between them seemed so supercharged. Celia had left a legacy of passion here. A year had passed before Daniel Stewart came looking for her, but now he couldn't wait to take up where they'd left off.

Well, he would have to wait. And wait, and wait. She took a deep breath. 'Your intentions are obvious enough,' she said. 'Now you can hear mine, because if I'm coming on this jaunt it's on my terms. I sleep in my own bunk, and you stay at the other end of the waggon, and any crossing over I make.'

'No meeting half way?' His lips were twitching, as though this was a joke, but she didn't smile, she was in earnest.

'Not unless I make the first move. This is how I see the situation.' She found she was waving her half-eaten sandwich at him, which took some of the dignity out of the argument, so she put down the sandwich and went on, 'This isn't Cyprus. This is my home town, my neighbourhood, and I'm a different girl here. And as far as this girl's concerned you and I met yesterday. We don't carry on from where we left off, because this is an entirely new set-up with very different rules.'

He gave a slight nod, perhaps he was seeing her point of view or perhaps he was agreeing with her, and she told him something else he would agree with. 'Oh, you're very attractive—you know that, don't you? If you weren't I wouldn't be coming on this trip, would I? But that's not to say I want you to make love to me within the next two days. It's not to say I'll let you make love to me.' Then she smiled herself, with a hint of promise. 'On the other hand, you did tell me you could get any girl within twenty-four hours, and you do have a bit longer than that, so now's your chance to prove it.'

He gave her rather an odd look and she drawled, 'You're not scared of the challenge, are you?'

'I don't think so.'

'Well, those are my terms.'

'Fair enough,' he said promptly, and of course he thought they would end up together. He thought she was giving an extra touch of excitement and provocation to their jaunt around the countryside, but he was confident that he couldn't lose.

Lucy had about another couple of hours' work on the table, then home and back here in the morning. 'What time do we start?' she asked.

'Early, I thought. How does seven o'clock sound?'

'I'll be here. And I think you should be thinking about getting back to the hotel for a good night's sleep. William's a big shire horse, you'll need to keep a firm hold on the reins.'

'I had figured that.'

He had a natural arrogance that showed through

the charm, and she would enjoy seeing him as a loser for once. She drawled, 'I hope you have strong wrists.'

'Strong enough. I don't let go easily.'

Lucy knew what he meant, but he wasn't putting any grips on her. 'Goodnight, then,' he said. 'Will you say goodnight to Mr and Mrs Partridge for me?'

'Of course. Don't you want any sandwiches? Or what about the cocoa?'

'Is that what it is?' He peered into a mug. 'You drink it,' he said. 'Build up your strength for your turn on the reins.'

He didn't kiss her goodnight, but he gave her a slow devastating grin that suggested all sorts of intimacies, and when the door of the workshed closed after him she breathed 'Phew!'

It would be hard to imagine a man more different from Celia's Howard than this one. Howard was a super person. Even if he was sometimes a little stuffy he was a man for a lifetime. Daniel Stewart might make an exciting lover and companion, and a fair-weather friend. He wasn't for Celia, and he certainly wasn't for Lucy. Lucy wouldn't dream of getting involved with him, much less of having an affair with him.

The house was in darkness when she got back home. The bridge party was over, the players had gone, and Maman was in bed and probably asleep. But as Lucy looked round the bedroom door her mother stirred and murmured, 'That you, dear?'

'Are you awake?'

There was more stirring and yawning, and Maman raised a head, in a pretty pink ribbon boudoir cap, and asked sleepily, 'Is anything the matter?'

'No, but I'll be gone early in the morning and I won't be back till Tuesday. I'm taking the gipsy waggon round the Cotswolds.'

'Are you?' Maman presumed it was a business stunt, all outings in the waggon up to now had been. The waggon was too flashy for her refined tastes and she didn't care for the gipsy connections. 'I do think that caravan is so vulgar,' she said. 'Like something from a circus.'

'How about me painting an advertisement on the side?' Lucy teased. 'Come to Partridge and Friis and get some colour in your life.'

'You might as well,' sighed Maman. 'What time will you be going?'

'I'll be leaving here about half past six.'

The beribboned head sank back on the pillow. 'Very well, dear, I'll see you on Tuesday. Celia phoned this evening and asked to speak to you, don't forget to ring her.'

'Sure.' Lucy bent to kiss her mother's cheek and Maman sighed again,

'Why can't you find a nice man like Howard?'

'There aren't that many of them about,' said Lucy, and while her mother was agreeing with her she thought—and there aren't many about like Celia's other one either.

'I've never had a moment's worry with Celia,' said Maman, smiling in the dim light that filtered in from the landing, and Lucy suppressed a shiver.

It was fairly late, coming up to eleven, but Celia would sleep better after a phone call from Lucy, who went downstairs now and dialled the number of the London flat.

Howard answered, managing to sound brisk and efficient even at this hour, but when she said, 'It's Lucy,' his voice warmed. He approved of the bond between the sisters, because Celia didn't make close friends very easily. Lucy heard him call, 'Dearest, it's for you. It's Lucy.'

'Hello,' said Celia, a moment later. 'We've arrived safe and sound. Did you find the parcel I left you? I got her a scarf that matched her suit,' Lucy heard her explaining to Howard. 'I took it over this morning.'

'Yes,' said Lucy.

'All right, is it?'

'It's all right. I wiped it clean.'

'She likes it,' said Celia brightly. 'And how are things? Any exciting plans for the next few days?'

'I'll be away on business until Tuesday.' If she even hinted at her plans Celia's façade of normality would crack, and Howard would be alarmed and alerted. 'Don't worry,' said Lucy, 'everything's working out down here. There are no suspicions and no fuss. He'll have left before you come home and he won't be looking Lucy up again.'

'That's nice,' said Celia. 'That sounds lovely. Take care, won't you?'

'Every care,' said Lucy. 'I won't see any more of him than I have to.'

'That's right,' said Celia. 'Oh, you are a clever girl.' She was laughing, her sweet soft laughter, when they said goodbye and hung up.

I hope I'm not being too clever, thought Lucy, wondering how much of Daniel she would see, and shutting her mind to the possibility of the situation becoming too hot to handle.

CHAPTER FOUR

THE little town was silent when they set off next morning, except for the sound of clip-clopping hooves on the tarmac of the empty road. Shops were shut, blinds were still drawn in houses and flats. It was Sunday and even the early risers were still in bed at seven o'clock.

Uncle Joe stood in the archway leading to the yard at the back of the shop, watching until they turned the corner, but Aunt Dolly hadn't put in an appearance. She had left a large picnic hamper and kept out of the way, and Lucy knew that she still wasn't happy about this. If they had driven off in a car, on holiday together, she would have waved them goodbye, but there was something dark and secret about the vardo.

The whole thing was a bit of play-acting really. Something different, the sort of thing that Daniel would enjoy. He had greeted Lucy, when she'd reached the shop, with a boyish enthusiasm, and she had immediately been drawn into the spirit of the game, petting the great shire horse, feeding it with the sugar lumps she had brought along, helping to harness it between the shafts of the waggon.

They both walked at William's head while the waggon trundled through the sleeping town. Daniel had the leading rein and Lucy strolled along beside him, and perhaps because it was so quiet they did no talking, but each time she caught his eye he would smile at her.

The early morning was pearl-like, with a soft lustre on everything that promised a beautiful day. Daniel, in brown slacks and brown and white check shirt, made a splendid king of the road; and Lucy had dressed the part in a red and black peasant skirt and blouse, tying her hair back with a scarlet kerchief.

'You look stunning,' Daniel had said when she'd stepped out of her car.

'This is my vardo outfit,' she'd told him. 'I wear this when we go to the fêtes and I do my fortune-telling. You don't look so bad yourself.'

It was a pity that it had to end in bitterness. It would have been better if she could have enjoyed it all, not getting involved with Daniel because he certainly was not her type, but staying friendly and parting amiably. Well, she would enjoy today, and forget for a while that she had to leave him determined never to come up against Lucy Friis again.

At the end of the long road that was the little town of Moreton Meadows, they took a left-forking lane, meandering into the Cotswold hills. Sometimes they faced a vista of miles and miles of open space, a patchwork of fields and trees, farms and houses, stretching out ahead of them. Sometimes they went through lanes that were enclosed by high trees almost meeting overhead, in a shimmering green tunnel through which the light filtered.

Lucy lived a few miles from here, she went through lanes like these in her little van most days, but everything was slowed down this morning. There was plenty of time to look around, to see the honeysuckle climbing over the hedges, the poppies in the fields. Strange that the elm plague seemed to have made so little difference to the countryside, except for skeletal clusters here and there. There were still trees everywhere: larches, birches, sycamores, oaks. It was still a green and pleasant land, and she sat beside Daniel, while William plodded briskly along, and felt contentment lapping over her.

They hardly talked at all, but the silences didn't matter. This was a lovely laziness and she was glad she had come, and she would probably come again with somebody else. Plenty of men would be willing to accompany her, although there was the problem of the bunks. Perhaps with a girl companion. Or alone. She might even come alone.

She gave a gusty sigh of satisfaction. 'Thank you for reminding me that vardoes need to get out on the open road. It wasn't fair, keeping it stuck on the lawn like that.'

'It wasn't,' he said, and a wild tomcat, thin and black as a tiny puma, streaked out of the hedgerow just in front of William's hooves, and Daniel's grip tightened on the reins, holding the horse back. Lucy had asked if he had strong wrists and he had. She was sitting so close that she felt the muscles harden in his arms.

She was a strong girl herself, healthy and vital, but she certainly couldn't have stopped William in his tracks so quickly. She had been jerked forward and she twisted in her seat, looking up at Daniel. 'You're a bit of a cheat,' she said.

'I am?'

'Well, you're deceptive.' He was tall, slim, almost willowy, but he must have mucles like steel. 'I wouldn't have thought you could have stopped William like that,' she said. 'You're *strong*.'

'And where's the cheating there? Did I say I wasn't?'

Her plan was developing a flaw. He could probably hold her down with one hand if he should turn angry, so when the showdown came she must make sure she was nowhere that was too lonely. Perhaps she shouldn't risk that second night. Tomorrow afternoon she would suggest they make for home, and tell him when they reached the cottage that although he was very good-looking he didn't turn her on. 'It's been fun seeing you again,' she'd say, 'and I hate to spoil your winning streak of any girl within twenty-four hours, but you're wasting your time here.' That should send him away and keep him away.

'That's a funny look you're giving me,' said Daniel,

and she sat back in her seat and frowned down at her hands, murmuring,

'What do you mean? What kind of a funny look?'

'A scared one.' That wasn't surprising. All of a sudden she was a little apprehensive. 'What bothers you about me being able to hold a horse back?' he asked.

'I'm not bothered, just surprised.' She bit her lip and tried to smile. 'Although it did just strike me that if you decide to break the rules I might find myself where I didn't want to be, and not able to do much about it.'

His laughter was a hoot of amusement. 'You mean you think I might take you by force, as the saying goes?'

It wasn't so far-fetched. It could happen. Lucy had always presumed she could look after herself, but it could happen, and she was unable to keep the acid out of her voice as she snapped, 'It would be about the daftest thing you ever did!'

'And the most unlikely.' All right, it had never happened. Celia had fallen for him on sight. That was the reaction he expected, and had apparently always got. Up to now. But this was going to be different, and Lucy said slowly, 'You say no girl's ever turned you down. Suppose one did?'

He shrugged, 'Then I'd put it down to experience. I don't go in for the rough stuff.'

No, she reassured herself, he was too cool-headed to lose his head. She couldn't imagine him risking anything that might be ultimately self-destructive, She said, 'Of course not. Sorry about the funny look.'

'Not at all, it was flattering. I'm sure you don't scare easily.' And then she was laughing too, because there hadn't been much fear in her life, although she was scared right now for Celia.

'Spiders,' she said. 'The great big harvest ones. Especially if they have fur on.'

Daniel chuckled. 'Well, I'm no spider, and I won't

break your rules. I won't take a thing that isn't offered.'
He lifted her hand to his lips, brushing the palm lightly,
and again she felt the prickling shock that was becoming
a reflex action every time he touched her. Each contact
gave her the same jolt, and there was no doubt that
physically Daniel Stewart was a powerfully disturbing
man. Then he smiled into her eyes, and tucked her hand
into the crook of his arm so that they sat closer together
than ever.

After the first few hours the cars were on the roads,
traffic building up even along the lanes as the morning
wore on. Sometimes they had to draw William to a halt
while cars, or cycles, or motorbikes, passed by. Sometimes they were perilously near the hedgerows, and Lucy
winced for her paintwork brushing against brambles
and overhanging trees.

They got curious startled faces peering at them
through car windows, cyclists stopping for a closer
look, and they brightened up Sunday for a couple of
villages.

At the first village a cricket match was being played
in a field, and when the waggon trundled into view
play stopped while the bowler watched them passing
by. Several children, sitting on the fence, keeping an
eye on the game, scrambled down and followed the
waggon; and everybody who saw them turned and
smiled, and often called to somebody else to come and
see.

'I feel like royalty,' Lucy laughed. She had driven out
to fêtes with Uncle Joe, and wherever it went the waggon created something of a stir. But today, in the sunshine, with Daniel handsome as the devil beside her,
there was a feeling of extra excitement, and of escape.
As though she wasn't Lucy Friis, hardworking career
girl, who knew more of less where she would be and
what she would be doing for the next twelve months,
but a Romany travelling where the road took her, her
man beside her.

The cars were a nuisance, but that was modern life. The waggon belonged to a vanished age, and it was fun, all of it, the sun beating down, the scent of grasses and wayside flowers.

Around midday they drew up, to give William a rest. Lucy opened Aunt Dolly's hamper and they ate bread rolls and cold chicken pieces and hunks of fruit cake, and drank from the flask of coffee she had included.

Aunt Dolly made delicious home-made wines, and it was the kind of hamper where you might have expected more in the liquid line than coffee and two bottles of milk. Lucy guessed that Aunt Dolly was anxious she should keep a clear head, and was inclined to agree that it would be stupid not to stay cold sober while they were driving along the lanes and through the villages and, for Lucy at least, sheer madness to risk anything that might blur her control and purpose when they had their evening meal and their long night together under the stars loomed ahead.

They followed the route on Uncle Joe's map, and the sun had set when they came to the five-barred gate that opened on to a wide cart track. This was where they were staying, in a field through which the river ran. Lucy had known the family living in the Cotswold farmhouse all her life. She had come over here sometimes as a child, playing in the fields, swimming in the river.

Once the river had run fast and deep enough to work a water mill—the farm was called Old Mill Farm—but that had been over fifty years ago. Now this tributary was silting up, although the water was still fresh and clear, and the ruined mill looked picturesque and eerie, with a flight of rooks from a nearby copse wheeling and cawing above.

'Is Dracula at home?' asked Daniel, looking across at the overgrown walls. Lucy had said. 'About here, I should think,' and he'd pulled on the reins and she'd jumped down to start unhitching William.

'He wasn't last time I called,' she said. 'It's the old water mill.'

'That's probably what they're putting around,' said Daniel.

'Doesn't it suit?'

'It's perfect.'

No one was likely to bother them here, even the farmhouse and buildings were out of sight on the other side of the copse. Freed of the shafts William immediately began to crop the lush green grass. It was good grazing land, the cows had been taken in for milking, but sheep and lambs were in the next field.

Lucy breathed the warm evening air, and stretched, hands on hips, rotating her shoulders, loosening muscles, and Daniel said, 'I know a better way.'

'I'll bet you do,' and she stiffened slightly as he pulled off the kerchief tied around her head, dropping it, running his fingers through her hair and gently kneading the back of her neck. She wanted it to go on, she could have purred like a kitten, but she wriggled loose.

'Nice,' she said, 'but I need to walk around for a while. Footboards aren't the softest seats.'

'Where are we walking?'

'Shall we call on Dracula?'

First they got William out of his harness, then they walked along the river bank towards the ruined mill. 'I haven't been here for ages,' Lucy said. 'There's a fishing stretch just round the bend in the river, I used to come with Uncle Joe and my father. They're not my uncle and aunt really, Joe and Dolly, but——'

'Did Celia come with you?'

She shot him a swift sidewards glance, but he was looking at the mill. When she didn't answer right away he half turned, half smiled, and she was pretty sure there was nothing in particular behind his question. 'Not often,' she said. 'My sister isn't really a country girl.'

'What a waste, living around here and not caring for country life.'

'That's not what I meant. I meant the farmyard stuff. Of course she likes living around here.' The meadow grass gave way to a narrow strip of stones and shingle, and Lucy stepped on the larger stones, eyes down, concentrating on where she was putting her feet. 'She has a lovely garden, better than ours because it's bigger, although ours is nice. My mother likes gardening. Do you have a garden or a window box or anything?'

'No,' he said. 'Is she like you?'

'My mother?'

'You told me your sister wasn't.'

Yes, she had, and she wanted to keep the talk away from Celia, so she launched into a description of Maman, which was loving but tinged with wry amusement.

There was no doubt which daughter was Maman's favourite, but Lucy had long ago grown accustomed to that. Her father had taught her to smile when the things that Celia did always met with more praise and approval. Even when they both got places in art college it was Celia for whom Maman saw the glowing future. And then of course Celia had married Howard and that, in Maman's eyes, had been the best of all possible decisions. Maman was a darling, but she was a snob, and Celia seemed to have been born with the social graces.

'My mother's a very elegant lady,' said Lucy. 'She's French and she has exquisite taste. She never quite got over the shock of finding herself married to my father, who owned half a shop and restored old furniture for a living. She doesn't care much for the vardo, she says it looks like something from a circus.'

She laughed at that, because of course it did, and Daniel asked, 'How do you get on with her? You don't seem to have much in common.'

'No, we don't,' and she went on smiling. 'But I wouldn't change her, I love her very much and she loves me, although there are ever so many improvements she'd like to see in me.'

'Such as?'

'Well, for one thing she'd rather I was a portrait painter. Or did flower studies. With a studio, not a workshed, and definitely not a stall on the market.'

'And that's not you?'

'Not at the moment, anyway.' Some time it might be a studio, but she enjoyed the auctions, hunting down old furniture and transforming it. She liked the market. 'Most of all,' she said, 'she'd like me to get married, like my sister did.'

'Celia.' Daniel said the name slowly, as though he was thinking about it as he spoke. 'And is Celia happily married?'

'Very. She has two children.' She could see them as she spoke, so dear to her and so vulnerable, and she wondered whether she should risk an appeal to Daniel even now. But it was a heck of a chance to take when she hadn't a clue how he would react.

He could think it was amusing—after all, he hadn't been hurt. But that wasn't to say he would keep quiet about it for the rest of his life, and nothing less than complete secrecy would save Celia's marriage. Howard had never forgiven his mother and he could well look on Celia's one lapse as an equal betrayal.

'Your mother wants you married and settled down, does she?' said Daniel.

They had reached the old water mill, where stone steps led to what had been the door. The great wooden wheel had vanished and the river ran shallow. With no roof, and with gaping windows, there was no clue to what the building had been.

'Not to any ordinary bloke,' said Lucy. 'She wants another son-in-law with status. Celia married our local M.P.'

He was probably going to learn that anyway, in the next few days, and then he might wonder why Lucy hadn't mentioned it. 'A politician?' He didn't sound impressed, voice and expression were cynical, and she asked,

'Don't you care for politicians?'

'I wouldn't put myself out for most of them.'

'At least they try.' Lucy was stung, because Howard worked hard. 'At least Howard does.'

'Is he a pillar of the establishment?' drawled Daniel, and she said shortly,

'Pillars are necessary. Especially when they're good strong straight pillars.' But at Daniel's grin her determination to keep him as far away as possible from Howard and Celia grew even stronger.

He pushed aside the creeper to peer into the shell of the mill, asking, 'And you do you get on with this famous brother-in-law?'

'He isn't exactly famous, but all right, why shouldn't I? Why do you ask?'

'Oh, the gipsy in you, the touch of the wild girl when the rest of your family seem so ultra-respectable. Including Joe and Dolly.'

'I'm no wild girl.'

'In Cyprus you were,' he said softly, and her cheeks flamed. It was a warm evening, and she was hot and sticky from the dust of the road, and she could feel the blush spreading until all her skin seemed to be burning. That was stupid, because she had never gone crazy for him, nor for anybody, and if she had been in Celia's shoes out there it would have been a different story.

'This is England,' she said tartly. 'I thought you realised that. I thought I'd mentioned it.'

'Sorry.' Daniel leaned closer, tracing her profile with a fingertip, but when he touched her soft quivering lips she jerked back her head, gasping,

'It's got worse since I was here last.'

'What has?'

'The mill. More overgrown.'

She went past him, ducking away from the creeper, through the doorway. This had once been a home as well as a mill, this had been the living room, but now little remained but stonework, some fallen beams, and the remains of a staircase leading nowhere.

'Nobody's home,' she said.

'Dracula will be lying low, the moon's not up yet.'

'I'm not sure that's funny.'

The empty cavern of the mill was rather weird in the half light, filled with rustlings and shadows, and when Daniel put an arm around her she said, 'There's no more to see. There used to be an upstairs when we were children.'

'Who's we?'

'Me and the Thornways, Sandra and Colin. The Thornways farm here.' She shivered. 'It's spooky, but if it is haunted it won't be Dracula, it'll be the poor old miller.'

'What happened to the poor old miller?'

'Nothing at all,' and she took the few steps that got her outside again, Daniel with her, his arm around her except for the moment when she stooped, to go through the doorway. As soon as they were down the steps he put a hand on her shoulder again. 'That was the trouble,' she said. 'He turned up for his wedding and the girl had run off with a soldier. He'd just come back from the Boer War and—well, that was it. The miller came back here and nothing ever happened to him, and he never left the mill again until he died, years later.'

'What of?' said Daniel. 'Boredom?'

'I always thought it was rather sad. It's true, you know. He turned into a hermit. He went on working the mill, but his life was over.'

Daniel didn't think it was sad. His expression was

amused bewilderment, and she asked, 'Don't you feel sorry for him?'

'He sounds a dead loss. The girl was well out of it.'

Perhaps it was a silly story, but it was a small tragedy too, and she wished he had said something like, 'Poor old chap!'

'I prefer Dracula,' and Daniel bowed his head, putting his mouth to her neck and biting it very gently.

'Talking of food,' she said, 'I think it's time for supper.'

His breath tickled, making her giggle. 'So do I,' and his tongue probed the convolutions of her ear.

'Good nourishing Aunt Dolly sustenance. I'm not on the menu.'

'Not even for afters?'

'Let's have supper first.' She had to go on playing with fire up to a point, as though she was giving him a chance to turn her on. 'I'll get it ready,' she said.

'You don't want to walk any further?'

It was a warm evening, a lovely evening, but Lucy didn't want Daniel's arm around her any longer. The last thing she needed was to find she was enjoying him touching her. 'You take your walk,' she said. 'You can walk right along the river here. Say about a quarter of an hour?'

'All right.' She left him there and when she looked back a few moments later he was walking away. He hadn't argued that he should be doing his share of the chores, he'd accepted her offer to prepare the meal and—presumably—set up camp for the night, while he wandered along the river bank. Spoiled rotten, she thought. Because he looks like somebody out of a sexy movie it's all laid on for him.

Of course he wasn't sorry for the poor old miller. No girl had ever left him at the church, or anywhere else. He'd be the soldier coming back, smiling and beckoning, with the miller's girl running right into his arms.

Lucy could have done with some help. Not that there was all that much to do, but she was beginning to feel jaded, and quite uncomfortably grubby, sticky with grime. She would have a wash just as soon as she had put things to rights.

She fixed the steps and went up into the waggon. The light was fading inside, dimming the colours in the painted woodwork, and the curtain pulled across the bunk blotted out the window at the end. She had brought a sleeping bag for Daniel, and she dragged it out of the long locker seat. The seat was too narrow to sleep on, so it was the floor or outside. That was up to him, but either would be pretty hard, and she grinned, savouring the thought of him sleeping rough and waking stiff.

The larder was a cupboard under the back of the waggon, and she got food out of there and from the basket, and set up the Primus stove outside. She washed in a little of the water, just her hands and a sprinkling for her face. In the morning she would go up to the farm and use their bathroom, but for tonight this would have to do.

It was almost too sultry to eat, and she set the meal outside on a big white cloth: crackers, butter, tomatoes, cheese, fruit. Then she took off her shoes and stockings, wriggling her toes in the cool grass, and sat waiting for Daniel to come back.

She wished he wouldn't. She would have preferred the night alone, or with less demanding company. Now the shadows were closing in, but instead of freshening up the air was getting more oppressive, and Lucy rolled over on to her stomach and buried her face in the cool grass.

She could have slept like this for a while, with everything blotted out, but she turned her head, resting it on her folded arms, because she wanted warning of Daniel's approach. She didn't want him flinging himself down beside her. She could find herself locked in his arms if she closed her eyes and let herself drift away.

When she saw him she sat up again, quickly. He walked with a loose stride, an almost animal grace, beside the river until he was level with the waggon, then coming up the bank on to the meadow. 'It's quite a night,' he said.

Rooks were still winging over the edge of the copse and soon there would be a great glowing moon. It was pale as yet, but the world would be bathed in moonlight tonight. 'Supper's ready,' said Lucy. She lit the gas and balanced the kettle, then sat watching the little blue flame, waiting for the water to boil, while Daniel moved around, in the waggon and around it, quiet-footed.

Often when he passed her he touched her, a light hand on her hair or fingers rippling down her bare arm, and she resented this claim to familiarity. She didn't return it, but she had to accept it because she had accepted his invitation to be here, and she was supposed to be the girl who had let him make complete love to her just a year ago.

Supper wasn't a hearty meal. Lucy had to force herself to eat, and Daniel didn't seem to be hungry. They played around with the food, and Lucy told him all about the family in the farmhouse and chattered about general things. She did most of the talking. He was a good listener, he put in the odd question to keep her rattling away, and perhaps he preferred half lying, propped against the waggon steps, more asleep than awake.

He was relaxed, all the long lean length of him, but Lucy sat, feet tucked beneath her, until her ankles ached and she had to ease them out and rub them. When the moon was up and the stars were out she looked across—at the end of a description of the Jubilee fête in Moreton Meadows when a cloudburst had coincided with the carving of the roasted ox, almost putting out the fire and leaving the roasters operating under dripping umbrellas—and Daniel's eyes were closed.

The moonlight made his face look pale and striking as a marble effigy: the high smooth brow, the fine straight nose with its flaring nostrils, the curved and sensual mouth; and she nearly bellowed, 'Hey, wake up!' at him. She didn't particularly want him awake, but it was exasperating to find that she had put him to sleep.

I'll leave him, she decided. I'll put the food away and fetch his sleeping bag out and get into my bunk. If I can step round without waking him. If I do wake him I'll say I'm tired, that I need my sleep too.

'We could do with some rain tonight,' said Daniel suddenly. So he had been listening, he wasn't sleeping, and she said,

'You've got your eyes closed,' sounding aggrieved.

His eyes opened. 'Am I missing something?'

'You looked as though you were asleep.'

'No.' He sat up. 'Is it all right for swimming?'

'Well, yes, but——'

She had never swum in the river in darkness, but there was moonlight enough to see by, and that was a reason she couldn't go swimming. 'I haven't brought a swimsuit,' she said.

'Does it matter?' He was unbuttoning his shirt, shrugging at her protests, reminding her, 'We have seen each other before,' and she knew what he was remembering and found it incredible. She couldn't imagine Celia naked before a man. Not even with Howard. From when they were children Celia had always insisted on having the bathroom to herself, and rushed for covering if she was caught unawares. She had asked for her own bedroom before they reached their teens, and Lucy had been moved into the box-room.

Celia was quite prudish in her modesty, and yet this

man would have expected her to run into the river, in the bright moonlight, and not bother about a swim-suit or anything. Lucy shook her head, and he thought that meant that she wasn't swimming, but what she really meant was—I can't believe it, I still can't believe it.

'Well, I'm going in,' he said.

He went into the waggon while she started to clear away the remains of the meal. He was out again in a couple of minutes, a towel knotted around his waist, and Lucy carried some of the food to the larder at the back of the waggon, and stayed there, giving him time to reach the river, drop the towel and get into deep water.

He was swimming a leisurely crawl when she rounded the waggon again, and she pushed back her hair because it was plastered to her forehead. The night was airless, muggy hot, and the grime of the day was gluing her blouse to her back. She didn't have a swimsuit, but she did have a change of bra and pants, she could swim in those, and she probably wasn't going to sleep tonight unless she cooled off somehow.

She dug out another towel from the linen drawer. Daniel had, of course, taken the biggest and best, but this would do. Then she got out of blouse and skirt and went down to the river bank, dropping this towel beside his.

The first chill of the water made her catch her breath. She shivered briefly, then ran splashing, strik-ing out in a breast-stroke. She and Celia both swam well and Daniel came swimming to meet her, shaking water from his hair, laughing, asking, 'Isn't it great?'

'Lovely.' It was cold and delicious, more refresh-ing than any shower or scented bath in a bathroom.

'Remember the last time we swam?' His teeth flashed in a smile and she said warily.

'I don't remember anything.' Celia hadn't told her about that. She didn't even know whether they had swum in the sea or in an hotel pool. If she simply said, 'Yes,' she would be taking a risk, so she said, 'I told you, we only met the day before yesterday,' and she began to swim towards the stretch round the bend in the river where her father and Uncle Joe used to fish.

Daniel kept pace with her, stroke for stroke. 'Then we're doing all right, aren't we?' he said, and she quickened her speed, wanting to get ahead, as though the naked man swimming beside her, sometimes brushing against her, was a predatory pursuer.

But she wasn't going to get away, because he was still there, still smiling, asking her, 'Is this a race?'

'No.'

'You've improved in the last twelve months.'

She dived shallowly, swimming under and coming up a little distance away, wondering what he was talking about. 'You're a much better swimmer tonight,' he called across the dark water, and she could only guess that Celia had pretended she wasn't so good. Girls often did, especially on holiday, when they wanted a good-looking man to teach them, to help them. It didn't sound like Celia, but then none of this did. 'Maybe I'm more at home in my native waters,' she called back.

'You're quite a cheat yourself, aren't you?'

That made her swallow a mouthful of river water, and she choked, spitting it out. 'Who isn't?' she said, and went on swimming.

When you rounded the bend, past the copse, you could see the lights of the farmhouse. It was some time since Lucy had been here, but she knew the house, and the farmer and his wife, and the brother and sister. Colin Thornett, a year older than Lucy, had gone out with her a few times, but she hadn't seen him for ages. It had been a boy-girl affair, well, not even that really, but they were a nice family, and inside the house everything would be safe and secure.

I must be mad, she thought, swimming out here in the dark with a man I know nothing about. Except that he takes photographs for a living and he managed to seduce Celia in Cyprus, and I'm sharing a waggon with him tonight.

She had a sudden urge to swim to the bank, get out of the water and run for the farmhouse, and ask if she could have a bed for the night. But all kinds of gossip would start if she did that. Instead of helping Celia she would have made sure the whole thing got broadcast far and wide, and all she had to do was get through tonight. She could go home tomorrow. She wasn't on the high seas or in the middle of the desert. She had a way out whenever she wanted it, but if her plan to get rid of Daniel was going to work she had to play it cool for a few more hours.

All the same she looked longingly at the lights in the farmhouse windows before she turned away and began swimming back. In spite of her energetic exercise the water had chilled her. Her teeth were chattering when she came out and she grabbed the large towel and huddled into it. She picked her way quickly and carefully over the strip of shingle and hurried across the grass to the waggon.

Daniel was just behind her, not more than a couple of paces. If he hadn't been she might have shut the door and bolted it, but she heard him following her and she stumbled to the far end of the waggon, where she had a nightdress and a cotton housecoat lying on the bunk.

He asked, 'Where are the matches?'

'On the d-dresser.'

'I'll light the lamp.'

She didn't want the lamp lit, until they were both dried and dressed; and she blotted hair, shoulders and breasts frantically with the big soft towel, slipping off the wet clinging bra straps, pulling the nightdress over her head and putting her arms into the housecoat.

She breathed a little easier then, and wriggled out of her pants, drying the rest of herself under the folds of the housecoat.

The lamp had begun to glow, but she didn't look at it, nor at Daniel until he said, 'That's clever.'

'What is?'

'How you dry a foot standing on one leg and wearing a tent.'

'My housecoat,' she said. It was white cotton, with wide sleeves and a full skirt, and she had packed it because it was a good cover-up. She was relieved to find him trousered, vigorously towelling his back. 'That was good,' she said. 'Wasn't it good?'

'Better than last year?' His grin was wicked and she said quickly,

'Different.'

'Shall I dry your hair?' He was moving towards her and if he pulled her down on the bunk she would probably have to fight to push him away.

'No, thank you,' she said crisply. 'I'll rub it dry myself, and I'll probably go over to the farmhouse in the morning and wash it. If you don't mind, I'm drawing the curtain now and getting behind it.'

'On your own?'

'That's right.' She kept her voice light, she didn't want a heavy scene. 'I warned you,' she said, 'I'm a different girl here.'

'Not my holiday girl at all?' His eyes were smoky grey in the lamplight—better than the steely glint she had seen occasionally, but they could still throw her into confusion. She pulled the curtains and turned to face him when he was close enough to touch her.

'Holidays are different, aren't they?' she said.

'Why?'

Stripped to the waist his shoulders seemed broader, his stomach looked flat and hard. His sheer physical good looks made a powerful impact so that she could have stared at him, and wondered about him, if circumstances had been different.

'Life's probably one long holiday for you,' she said, and he didn't deny it. 'But here, where I live, I have to like a man very, very much before I'd want him to even kiss me.'

'And you don't like me very, very much?'

She didn't like him at all. If he'd been about half as good-looking, half as sure of himself, he might have been the kind of person she liked. But she said, 'So far I like you. Let's see if the very, very comes later. Tomorrow maybe.'

She wouldn't have been surprised to find herself struggling. With the bunk just behind her, and Daniel so close that he could have pushed her backwards with an outstretched hand, it wouldn't have surprised her if he had tried physical persuasion, and she was relieved that he didn't.

He didn't even touch her. What he did do was say, 'On a night like this I wouldn't mind sleeping outside,' and she said,

'Neither would I. It's stuffy in here.'

'You're welcome to share my sleeping bag.'

She yawned and laughed, 'I think if I want any rest I'd better stay with my bunk.'

'Goodnight, then.'

'Well, goodnight.'

It was that easy, which was fine because she was tired. Daniel took the sleeping bag out under his arm, and after a moment or two she shut the door, upper and lower sections, and slid the bolts as quietly as she could. She didn't want him changing his mind about anything in the small hours, but if he did he would have to knock to get into the waggon, and that would have her up and wakeful.

The window behind her bunk seemed to be stuck, but as she had the waggon to herself she could have the curtain open, and although it was still a sweltering night she fell asleep without too much trouble.

She woke a couple of times, once when an owl hooted, so close that she shot upright, convinced that the bird was in the waggon, and once when even a single sheet weighed too heavily and she had to throw it off. But each time she snuggled down again, and the next thing she heard was the chorus of early morning birdsong.

She smelled bacon cooking, and peering through a side window saw Daniel's back. He was squatting over the stove. 'Morning!' she carolled. 'What time's breakfast?'

'Right now,' he said. 'How many eggs?'

'One, please.' The sky was a flat grey, which could be for heat again or might be for rain. Lucy got out her overnight bag, grimaced at her reflection in the make-up mirror, and moved fast with cleansing lotion on a pad of cotton wool. A slick of lipstick was all the make-up she had time for right now, and no amount of brushing was going to turn her hair into a shining glory until she'd washed the sticky residue of river water out of it.

But she was opening the door, dressed and fairly presentable, in about three minutes, feeling quite pleased with herself until she saw Daniel. He looked as though he had shaved, his skin looked cool and smooth and he made her feel even scruffier than she was.

'How long have you been awake?' she demanded.

'I wake early.'

'Guilty conscience?'

'Who, me?' The dark brows arched. 'Why should I have a guilty conscience?'

Because he was one of the lucky ones, a natural heart-breaker. 'I don't know,' she said, as she came down the steps. Bacon was still frying. Some was on a plate, he had put more in the pan when he knew she was up. 'Did you tell me much about yourself?' she asked.

'Don't you remember?'

That had been a risky question, but if there had been anything very dramatic and memorable Celia would surely have mentioned it. 'You take photographs,' she said, 'but for the life of me I can't remember much else. Like, have you been married?'

'No,' he was very emphatic about that.

'Against it, are you?'

'For me I am.' He stabbed bacon with a fork, turning it as it spluttered. 'And I remember you saying how much you valued your freedom, so why are you looking so disapproving?'

'I'm not,' but she had thought it was typical of him, avoiding commitments and responsibilities, and if Celia had said that Lucy very much hoped it was part of the silly game she was playing. Surely Celia had all the freedom she needed. She wanted for nothing, and if she had run down marriage when she was talking to Daniel twelve months ago she was desperate now to save her own marriage.

'I'm going over to the farm after breakfast,' said Lucy. 'I could do with a bath after last night's swim.'

'Good idea,' said Daniel, 'I'll join you.' When her eyebrows lifted he grinned, 'Two baths, if they can run to them.'

She supposed it would be all right, arriving around breakfast time and asking if they might take over a bathroom for half an hour or so, although she would have preferred calling on her own. It wouldn't have seemed quite such an imposition.

She said, 'Let's wait till the workers are through, shall we?'

Just after nine o'clock they walked through the little copse towards the farmhouse, being hailed by two big light-haired ruddy-complexioned men as they approached, both calling, 'Hello, Lucy.'

'It's Mr Thornett and Colin.' She quickened her step. 'How are you? You're both looking very fit.'

'And so are you,' said Mr Thornett. 'Great,' said

Colin, who had had a soft spot for Lucy ever since she
had joined in the haymaking, and roamed the fields and
hills, when she was brought over here on her father and
Uncle Joe's fishing expeditions.

Father and son were looking at Daniel now, as though
he wasn't quite what they had expected, and Daniel
said, 'Thanks for letting us pitch here.'

'Any time,' said Mr Thornett.

The kitchen curtain moved and a few moments later
Sandra Thornett, Colin's sister, a year younger than
Lucy, a brown-eyed, brown-haired girl, came out of the
house. They had all been curious, since Joe Partridge's
phone call, to see who Lucy would be turning up with,
and first sight of Daniel Stewart had had Sandra gog-
gling.

But by the time she joined them she was simply smil-
ing a welcome. 'Hello, Lucy, it's nice to see you again.
Pleased to meet you,' she said when Lucy introduced
Daniel. 'Are you new in these parts?'

'I'm here on holiday,' said Daniel, and Lucy knew
that Sandra was getting a thrill from the sexy voice, and
the smile turned on her as though she was someone
special.

'Oh, are you really?' said Sandra, as though that *was*
clever, being here on holiday, and Lucy asked,

'Would it be all right if I had a wash?'

'Yes, of course, come on in.' The two farmers said
their cheerios, Colin rather reluctantly, and strode off
towards their day's work, and Sandra led Lucy and
Daniel through the backdoor into the farmhouse, asking Lucy, 'You know where the bathroom is, don't
you?'

It was in the same place it had been years ago, and
Lucy wasted no time, washing herself and shampooing
her hair, though it didn't matter much if Sandra and
Mrs Thornett were asking Daniel where he came from
or how long he'd known Lucy. They wouldn't know she
hadn't been to Cyprus last year.

She towelled the dripping wetness out of her hair, shook her head vigorously, and came back downstairs to the kitchen, where Daniel and Sandra and her mother were all sitting at the table, drinking tea.

'I hope you don't mind,' said Lucy, 'but I used some of your shampoo.'

'That's all right,' said Sandra. She didn't take her eyes off Daniel and they were all smiling.

'Have a cup, Lucy?' suggested Mrs Thornett, starting to pour.

'Thank you.'

'We were talking about the day you walked across that plank and fell in the creosote vat,' giggled Sandra, and Lucy pulled a face.

'I'll never forget it!'

'She used to be a real tomboy,' said Mrs Thornett, 'when they used to come up here, your father and Joe Partridge. I remember trying to clean you up that day before they took you home, and your father saying how your mother would create "a fuss" because it was a new pair of jeans and a new jumper you were in. He said she'd say, "Nothing like this ever happens to Celia".'

She went on chuckling, leaning back in her chair, remembering old times, and Sandra said, 'Do you know Celia, Lucy's twin?' in case Daniel wasn't getting the point.

'You and Celia are twins?' Lucy felt his sharpened interest and said brightly,

'Yes, we are. It isn't that unusual, there are a lot of twins about. We're quite different—'

'Except in looks,' Mrs Thornett insisted. 'You're very alike, in looks.'

'Well,' said Daniel, 'that settles it.'

'Settles what?' The smile was fixed on Lucy's lips and her fingers felt stiff around the teacup.

'Now,' he said 'I *shall* have to stay and meet Celia.'

CHAPTER FIVE

IT was every bit as hot as yesterday, but today there were clouds, keeping out the sun but holding down the heat like a great grey blanket, and Lucy was developing a faint headache.

The niggle had started when Daniel said he would be staying to meet Celia, because that wasn't on; Celia wasn't up to it, which meant that very soon now there would have to be a sharp and final parting of the ways between him and Lucy. The anticipation was worse than the dentist's waiting room, jogging along, acting as though she hadn't a care in the world, tossing and combing her hair to dry it, and wondering how she was going to engineer the explosion.

'You don't turn me on, goodbye,' was what she had planned to say, but Daniel would have to make a fairly determined pass at her before she could tell him to hit the road, and he hadn't.

He'd put an arm around her as they sat together on the footboard, behind the horse, but even then he'd asked, 'Is this allowed?' and she'd had to say,

'Why not?'

'If you won't take a kiss unless you're very, very fond I wondered how touching rated.' He was mocking her, and she said stiffly,

'That depends.'

'Well, it would. On the how and the where.' His eyes were a touch that she felt on her breast, through the barrier of her blouse, and she said,

'I can stand a friendly arm around me, so long as I can move away when I want to.'

'Just say the word,' he said, 'and I'll tell the horse. We don't want you leaping into the ditch.'

William was going very slowly this morning, plodding sluggishly along, and all yesterday's gaiety seemed to have gone. Lucy wondered if Daniel was turning over in his mind about her and Celia being look-alike twins. It was bound to make him think, and if he tried he could trap Lucy on Cyprus any time. If he challenged her outright she would have to say, 'No, it wasn't me, but unless you want to smash up a home and a marriage and the lives of four or five people keep away from Celia. She doesn't want to see you. It was just a holiday affair that she bitterly regrets, because she isn't like that at all.'

But he didn't talk about Cyprus, nor about Celia. He talked about the Thornetts. He asked her, 'Are you fond of Colin?'

'I suppose so, yes.'—When they were leaving she had said, 'Tell Coll I'm sorry we only had time for a few words,' and Sandra had replied with, 'He hasn't got a steady, you know. Why don't you give him a ring some time?'—'But that,' said Lucy now, 'was because Sandra fancied you and thought it would be handy if I got back with Colin.'

'Got back with him?'

'We went out together, about half a dozen times. Ages ago. Years ago, while I was still at art school. I haven't seen any of the Thornetts for ages.'

'Shall you ring him?'

'No.' She had outgrown Colin. She had changed. It seemed a long time since she was eighteen, longer than four years.

'Was he the kind of lover you remember?' Daniel asked.

It had been a fumbling, mumbling affair, with Colin almost completely inexperienced and Lucy anxious not to commit herself in any way. They had never been real lovers, but she said, 'Yes.'

'Do you remember how it was with me?'

She could imagine, and she turned away so that he

couldn't see her face. 'Of course,' she said.

'That's something.' She could imagine his expression, he was smiling, and she said tartly,

'Don't they all remember you? You're the expert, aren't you, who can get any girl within twenty-four hours?'

A car went slowly by. There was much less traffic in the lanes today. The weekend travellers were at work and the heavy stuff kept to the better roads. The car driver and his passenger stared at the waggon and Daniel raised a saluting hand as they passed. 'You get around, don't you?' he said to Lucy.

He thought she was a wild one. He thought there was Cyprus and there was Colin, and she muttered, 'Do I?'

'Apparently. I don't know who told you he could get any girl in twenty-four hours, but it certainly wasn't me.'

She jerked round in her seat, her silky-fine still-damp hair getting in her eyes so that she had to blink. 'Are you sure you didn't?'

'Sure as can be,' said Daniel promptly.

'Oh! Well, I suppose you should know. It must have been someone else, then.' He must have forgotten. It was probably said as a joke, but Celia had reason to remember because Daniel had seduced her within hours. 'Look,' said Lucy, 'I think I've had enough of the gipsy life. Today isn't quite what it was yesterday and perhaps I'm a fair-weather Romany. So how about turning back, or if you don't want to do that will you put me down on a bus route?'

'I'm sorry. You're not enjoying it?' He sounded genuinely concerned, but she had been an idiot to come, and today *wasn't* like yesterday. There was a feeling about it of something horrid brewing. Trouble or storm. She had grumbled yesterday about the cars and cyclists, but today the lanes were almost deserted, and even the cattle and sheep in the fields huddled motionless. Today was a gloomy day.

'Shall we find a pub,' Daniel suggested, 'and have a good lunch.'

'We've food enough aboard to feed us for a week.'

'You don't really want to go back?'

Lucy didn't want to go on, because if it started to rain he wouldn't sleep outside and she felt her headache building up at the prospect of being shut in the little waggon with him all through the long dark night. 'I'd like to have reached the Dancing Stones,' he said. 'And I need a guide. It wouldn't be the same without you.'

The Stones were on Uncle Joe's map, on the farm where they were supposed to be staying for the night. There was a barn there for William, if the weather was bad, and when they arrived Lucy could say, 'I got claustrophia last night,' and they'd let her sleep in the house.

'Oh, very well,' she gave in grudgingly, and he smiled the sweet warm smile that covered a ruthless determination to get his own way.

She was sure that people always did what he wanted. He expected it and they did. Well, she would go to the Stones, it would be easier, taking the lanes and letting William amble on, then detouring into a town from which she might get a bus or taxi. But Daniel's hopes for tonight would come to nothing. If he had been the last man alive she wouldn't have let him love her.

He put an arm round her shoulders again, and she tensed slightly and he asked, 'What is it?'

'Thinking of the Stones,' she explained. 'They give me the shivers unless the sun's shining, and sometimes even then.' Of course it was him taking hold of her that had made her flinch, but it was true that the Stones were a strange and sinister place.

They stood on the top of a hill, a long hard haul from the village below; and Lucy and Daniel left

the waggon in a field, and William with his nose in
a manger, contentedly munching, and climbed the hill
on foot.

The clouds hadn't broken and the rain hadn't come,
but the whole landscape was bathed in a livid light,
a foreboding of storm, and the farmer's wife had
warned them, 'We're in for a downpour,' when they'd
said they were climbing up to the Stones.

'How do you feel about it?' Daniel had asked Lucy.
'I'm going up, but——'

'I don't mind the rain,' she'd said, 'and now I've
come this far I might as well.'

They went up the hillside, skirting a golden field
of corn and another of bright yellow rape, and she
let him take her hand, her arm, and lift her over a
stile, although she would rather have climbed the stile
unaided and walked without touching.

Everything was so still. There wasn't a breath of air.
Even on the hilltop not a leaf moved in the trees, and
the grey stones stood still and sullen under the lower-
ing sky.

Often, when you came up here, there were sightseers
about. Although it was on private land the farmer
turned a blind eye most of the time, but there was nobody around now. Lucy said, 'Well, here we are. This
is it.' In the middle of the field was a rough ring of
ancient weather-worn rocks, all shapes and sizes, and
another much smaller cluster a little way away. 'The
Dancers,' she said. 'They danced when they shouldn't
and so they were turned to stone. By them,' she nodded
towards the smaller group.

'And who turned them to stone?' asked Daniel.

'I don't know.' She grinned wanly. 'Maybe the
wizards weren't as smart as they thought they were.
Maybe the spell backfired. I don't like it much up here,
I never did. It's a strange place.'

'How strange?' Daniel stood with folded arms, sur-
veying the scene, and Lucy moved a little nervously,

a few steps first this way then that. She always found it hard to stand still up here.

She said, 'If you count them you never get the same number twice. Well, if you went on counting you would do, of course, but half a dozen people can count, separately at the same time, and come up with different answers. I'll bet if we did now our figures wouldn't be the same.'

'Let's see,' said Daniel. 'Let's start here.' He touched the first stone and went off clockwise round the circle, and after standing biting her lip for a moment Lucy walked in the other direction. She counted scrupulously, passed Daniel half way, and came back to the starting point more or less as he did. 'Thirty-eight,' she announced.

'Forty-one,' said Daniel.

'It always happens. I think they move, in a different time dimension from ours.'

'I wouldn't put it past them.' He was laughing at her, and she said,

'We don't know what they were put here for, do we? There are fairy tales about dancers being turned to stone, but these were always stones, weren't they? Only much much bigger than they are now, when somebody dragged them to the top of this hill thousands of years ago. And we don't know why, but I don't suppose it was for a pretty reason.'

'I don't suppose it was,' Daniel agreed

'If you stand in the middle,' said Lucy, 'and close your eyes, you can feel them coming closer. And you can hear them. When they get very near you can hear them breathing.'

'Is that the legend?'

'No, that's what I'm telling you. The middle's where you're supposed to stand and make a wish. You shut your eyes and wish. You always do, don't you, in these places? That's part of the fairy tale.'

'Do the wishes come true?' He was still humouring her, and she said,

'So they say, I wouldn't know. I've never wished because I can always feel the Stones coming to take me away and then I always open my eyes.'

She wasn't joking. She *had* always felt there was terror in this place, so strongly that the ritual of standing in the heart of the circle with closed eyes had been horrific to her as a child. She had always cheated, looking under lowered lids.

'Are you wishing today?' asked Daniel.

'Are you?'

'Of course. Come on, we'll stand together.' He walked into the middle of the ring and she followed him. 'Close your eyes,' he said.

As she did the wishes gabbled through her mind ... I wish you'd go away. I wish you'd go without seeing Celia. I wish you'd never come back ... And suddenly a wave of inexpressible desolation swept over her and her eyes flew open.

Daniel was watching. He had been curious, he'd wanted to see how she would react, and she almost shouted, 'No, I am not psychic, but yes, this place does give me the creeps!'

'It does, doesn't it?'

'May we go now? Is it all right if we go? Have you seen all you need to see?' She was blaming him, although it was hardly his fault that her head was throbbing and she felt sick.

'Are you all right?' His frown was worried. He put an arm around her, a hand cupping her chin, while his eyes searched her face. 'You're looking pale.'

'My head aches,' she said. 'It's the weather. And this beastly place. Abandon hope, that's how it always feels to me.'

Lucy had never been abandoned in her life. Even when her father died she had had family and friends around her, but here, just now, it had felt as though she hadn't a friend in the world.

Daniel was kind—at any rate he put on a show of consideration. He took her back down the hill, and made a strong cup of tea in the waggon, and while she drank that he went over to the farmhouse and returned with some parecetamols.

'The lady had migraines,' he said. 'She's sorry you've got a headache.'

'This isn't a migraine.' It was the nervous headache that had been lurking in her skull all day, but that last half hour had turned it into pounding pain.

'Take them anyway,' Daniel advised. 'They don't seem to have done her any harm.'

Mrs Rollins weighed a good fifteen stone and Lucy giggled as she swallowed the pills.

'Now try to sleep,' said Daniel, and that was exactly what she felt like doing so she lay on the bunk, and she didn't protest when he sat down beside her and began to stroke her forehead and temples, because it was comforting and his touch was cool. She heard rain start to patter overhead and Daniel talked, very quietly, for a while, telling her that she was relaxing and the pain was going and everything was all right.

He was no threat then. There was nothing sexual in this caress, and the gentleness was touching in one who seemed so self-centred. The pills made her muzzy, of course, and the rain was a soothing lullaby, and soon she was sleeping as soundly as though she was in her own bed at home.

When she woke the headache had gone, and she stared at the dark barrel-shaped roof above her for a few seonds before she realised where she was. Then she sat up and Daniel asked, 'Feeling better?'

He was sitting, feet up, on the long settee at the other end of the waggon, and Lucy said, 'Much better. I could paint the ceiling when I get back. Night or day, which do you think? Which would you like, stars or a blue sky and the sun shining?'

He leaned back to look up, and his throat and jawline looked smooth and hard, and she would have liked to run her fingertips along his jaw. 'Stars, I think,' he said. 'How long will it take you?'

Longer than he would be around. He wasn't going to see what she painted, so why was she consulting his preferences? He looked like a Regency poet, sprawled there, thick waving hair slightly dishevelled, shirt open to the waist, showing a shadow of hair on his chest.

'Is it Byron or Shelley?' she asked. 'The one you look like,' and he grinned.

'It's my father, actually, and he never wrote a line of poetry. I'd be surprised if he ever read one.' He'd said he had no family and she didn't think she wanted to hear about them because he would be gone within a matter of hours, never—please God—coming back. She didn't need to know his background, but all the same she said,

'My father died two years ago. How long——'

'Nearly five.'

'And your mother?'

'The same time.' It had to be a road accident, and she had probed a deep and painful wound, and she said,

'I'm sorry,' although it was impossible to tell what Daniel was thinking behind the handsome mask of his face. She began to babble. 'I took over my father's half of the business. It had been arranged I should work there, we'd planned that, I was going to do what I'm doing now. But he was going to be there too, of course, that was how we'd planned it.'

He said quietly, 'You told me. In Cyprus.'

'I did?' Celia had got into the skin of her part, this was real Method acting, and Lucy felt a shiver run down her spine, like hearing that someone had come across her *doppelganger*. What *had* possessed Celia? It might have been a joke if she hadn't let it develop into a full physical affair, but that wasn't a joke, that was appalling. 'I'd forgotten I told you,' she said.

'Now I sold the family business,' said Daniel.

'Oh? What was it?'

'A bit of land, a few houses. It brought in enough to keep me going.' He swung his legs off the settee, stood up and stretched, and Lucy squirmed to the edge of the bunk herself, enquiring,

'So you've got an income? You don't have to rely on your photographs for a living.'

His grin was mischievous. 'And why are you suddenly concerned with my finances?'

'I'm not,' she denied indignantly. 'I'm just talking, just thinking that you look somehow as though you were born with a silver spoon in your mouth. And as though you'd flog it as soon as you got your hands on it.'

'Wouldn't you?' he said. 'On that market stall of yours.'

She had to laugh. 'Anybody else's family silver, but not my family's. I'm a romantic about some things.'

'You want to watch that. It's an expensive luxury.'

'Oh, I watch it,' she said cheerfully. 'I ration it.'

'What to? High days and holidays?' It was trivial talk, but when he said 'holidays' she said,

'Was that how it was in Cyprus? A sentimental interlude?' She didn't really want to know, but it was such a mystery that she couldn't help asking, and he said,

'I wouldn't have said so. You didn't strike me as being overly sentimental.'

'Not even in Cyprus? How did I strike you?'

'As a beautiful woman.'

'Thanks.' Her voice was dry. 'And available?'

'Well, yes.' No wonder he was looking surprised, this kind of forgetfulness was very peculiar. Lucy picked up her hairbrush from the top of the chest of drawers and began to brush her hair until it crackled.

'I haven't given it that much thought,' she said, 'and

I'm sure you haven't either, but—'

'You're going to get another headache if you go on battering yourself,' he drawled, and she slowed down on the brushing. 'Now what are you asking me and why are you angry?'

'I'm not angry.' Of course she was incensed by Celia's lies and the tangle that was being spun around her. 'But I never expected to see you again,' she said. 'After all, what was it in Cyprus?'

'A pleasant encounter?' he suggested.

'Nothing really, was it?'

'Not a great deal,' he admitted, smiling as he agreed with her, and she had a brief flare of hope that Celia might have exaggerated. But of course Celia and Daniel had different life-styles. They had slept together, Celia had told her that, and although it had meant nothing much to Daniel it was something that Howard would never forgive.

'Why did you come looking for me, after a whole year?' she asked, and a few seconds passed before he answered. Then he said,

'I was in the hotel, looking at a local newspaper, and I saw your advertisement—Partridge and Friis. So I walked round to the shop.'

'You didn't come to Moreton Meadows because I had a shop there?'

'No.'

She began to laugh. 'I'll bet you never gave me a second thought until you saw my name.' The advertisement went in each week. If it hadn't Daniel Stewart, who just happened to be in the Cotswolds, like thousands every year, would probably never have bothered Celia again.

When he smiled and didn't deny it she said, 'That isn't very flattering,' her lips still curved in barely suppressed amusement.

'Do you want to be flattered?'

'Let's have the truth,' she said gaily. 'If it hadn't

been for that ad. I'd never have seen you again.'

'I might have walked through the market, and found you there, behind your stall.'

Rain beat steadily on door, roof and windows, and she could hear the thudding of her heart, louder in her ears than the rain, at the narrowness of that escape. If he had hailed her familiarly, with no warning, no briefing from Celia, she would have thought he was trying to pick her up, and she would have been cutting cool, distrusting his kind. Then when he reminded her that they'd met in Cyprus she would have laughed, 'That wasn't me. That was my twin, Celia.' No,' he would have said. 'Not Celia. Lucy.' And by then Ma Morris and Mavis, at least, would have been enthralled.

Still, it hadn't happened that way, and she was relieved to hear that the meeting had been casual rather than planned. She need not have worried about him remembering Celia too clearly either, because he'd hardly remembered her at all. 'I suppose we ought to eat,' she said.

'What is there?'

The only place he could stand upright was in the centre of the waggon, and even there his head almost touched the top. Aunt Dolly's hamper was in the floor space between the black unlit stove and the chest of drawers, and Daniel went down on his heels to open it. 'There's more in the larder at the back,' said Lucy. We might as well get it all out, I can't take it back home, and if we should need any more there'll be a shop tomorrow.'

She pulled out the small table while he was exploring the larder box, outside in the rain, and almost covered the table with the remains of Aunt Dolly's picnic. Among other things he brought in a tin of tomato soup, and they heated that and drank it from mugs, then piled their plates high with an assortment of left-overs.

It was a cosy meal, with the lamp burning and the rain a gentle pattering now. The table fronted the far end of the long settee, and it was a comfortable seat and Daniel was good company. They laughed a lot— just as he and Celia must have done. Lucy remembered her voice on the tape: 'We had something called mézé, there must have been about thirty dishes ...' Celia had been smiling to herself when she'd said that, although later on the tape she had been almost weeping.

Daniel said, suddenly and surprisingly, 'What's mézé got that this hasn't?'

'What?' She looked at him with startled eyes and he repeated,

'Mézé. You do remember the mézé?'

'Of course I do.' But her smile was twitchy, because it was almost as though he had read her thoughts. All he had done, of course, was remark on the number of dishes at that moment. A coincidence, and she was silly to be jumpy. She said, 'I bet we've got as many plates, even if the food isn't as exotic.'

'Think not? What are those strange-looking objects?' He pointed a fork towards a jar and she said,

'Pickled walnuts, you great ignoramus.'

'You hear that?' He appealed to the air around them. 'I've been nothing but civil to her and she's calling me names!' He reached for the jar and took off the lid. 'Your Aunt Dolly has done us proud. She's a very hospitable soul.'

'They both are.' They were the kindest of people, and Lucy added, 'But don't you get the idea they're a couple of simple-minded country folk.'

'Why should I?' He speared a small walnut. 'You don't run that business single-handed, and I should think Joe Partridge is nobody's fool.'

She gave an embarrassed little wriggle because the last thing she had intended was to sound superior. It was the last thing she felt. Uncle Joe was an astute

business man, and without him she might still have
been struggling to make a living. She said, 'You didn't
let me finish. I was going to say, "Don't think they're
simple-minded country folk because Aunt Dolly seems
to have taken to you." As a rule she's not easy to impress, but she thinks you look a well-set-up, clean-
living young man, and she likes your manners. The
way you carry trays, things like that.'

'I was nicely brought up,' said Daniel solemnly, and
Lucy murmured,

'With all those silver spoons?'

'They were a help, of course.'

'Of course.' She was laughing, but the next bit she
meant. 'All right, you were nicely brought up, but
I've got a hunch you're tougher than old boots.'

Behind the handsome smiling face there was that
feeling of steel. 'That's the gipsy in you,' said Daniel
lightly. 'You can't take anything at face value.'

'I'm not a gipsy.'

'You tell fortunes, don't you?'

'At the church fêtes? I make 'em up as I go along.'

He pushed aside his plate, the pickled walnut still
on the fork, and said, 'Tell mine.'

'All right.' It was always a lark, a party piece. Lucy
rubbed her hands together, getting down to the task.
'Now, if I'd known you were going to ask me I'd
have brought along the crystal ball or a pack of cards.
As I've got neither it's either tea-leaves or read your
palm. And, as the tea's all tea-bags, your hand, sir, if
you please.'

Daniel offered his right hand, and she placed it,
palm up, on the table, and bowed her head over.
Usually she held hands, she didn't stop to wonder
why she wasn't holding his, nor even touching it. She
stared down at the long fingers, well shaped, well mani-
cured, and started her patter about lines of heart and
head and life. So far as she knew—she'd read a book on
it out of the library before they took the vardo to the

first fête, and she first played the fortune-teller—they all looked fine. She pointed out the success line, running from the wrist straight up the palm, and the lucky-in-love sign, rising from inside the life line on the Mount of Venus. She always gave a glowing fortune and she did now. And wondered what she might have learned if she had had a genuine gift.

He knew she hadn't, that it was all a joke, and when she looked up and sat back he said, 'Very comforting. I shall face the future with real confidence now.'

'You've never been short of confidence,' she said with certainty.

'Is that part of the reading?'

'Part of the hunch.' She couldn't tell his future, but she could tell his character. He looked what he was, she was sure. 'You've got it made, haven't you?' she commented.

'Got what made?' He leaned closer, giving her a smouldering look like a take-off of an old-time movie love scene, and she grinned.

'Not me, so you can stop leering.'

'No? All right. Now let me read your hand.'

'You can't tell fortunes. Can you?'

'That's rich, coming from someone who makes them up as she goes along.' But when he reached for her hand she put them both behind her back and said, half seriously, 'I've got a bit of a complex about my hands.'

'What's wrong with them? Do you bite your nails?'

'Not much, no, but hauling furniture about you get broken nails, and the paint isn't very good for them either.'

He dragged one forward, and she grimaced. 'They are not a lady's hands,' she said with a faint French accent, explaining, 'My mother says that. She sighs about them. I did used to bite my nails when I was a child, I suppose that's what started her off. She has very beautiful hands. She always wears gloves for any sort of work, gardening, washing up, and she can't see why I can't wear gloves for my work, and grow my nails to an elegant length like she does.'

Daniel snorted. 'I never heard such rubbish! They're lovely hands, pretty and clever, what more does she want?'

'Long nails.'

'Does she expect you to scratch your designs?' He held her hand, but he looked at her face, as though he was reading that. 'You'll do all right,' he said.

'Promise?' Lucy felt lit from within with something that made her bright-eyed and glowing.

'We can't lose, can we?' he said. 'Either of us. It's writ in the stars.'

'Not tonight it isn't,' she said. The windows were shiny wet as the rain fell steadily from a jet black sky.

'Finished eating?' asked Daniel.

'Yes.'

'Come on, then, let's clear up.'

They scooped left-overs together and stacked dishes, and when Daniel opened the door, and picked up a pile of plates and the two mugs, Lucy stared. 'Where are you taking them?'

'I'm putting them out on the grass. They'll be clean by morning.'

'Yeuk!' she shuddered.

'Well, nearly.'

He went into the rain and she stood in the doorway, shaking with laughter as he arranged them around. 'I don't know about being nicely brought up,' she called, 'you've got some funny habits!'

'This isn't a habit.' He came in, hair glistening, shirt sticking across his shoulders. 'This was an inspiration. If it works it could become a habit.'

'I shouldn't bother patenting it,' she gurgled, and he said smugly,

'That's the trouble with you artists. You're all the same. You're just not practical. Now what shall we have for the first part of the evening's entertainment, music or talk?'

Lucy had brought her transistor radio along, and he picked it up and began twiddling knobs.

They had both. Sitting on the long settee, Lucy snugly tucked within Daniel's encircling arm, they listened to records claiming to be the best of jazz, and then to a fairly ingenious thriller-play. And time passed very comfortably until the National Anthem was played.

It was too late then to go over to the farmhouse and ask if they could put her up, but somehow she was neither embarrassed nor apprehensive. It had been like an evening spent with an old friend. She was at ease, and pleasantly weary.

When the radio was switched off, and there was silence, she realised how tired she was and yawned widely and stood up. 'I shall sleep like a log,' she announced.

'You will?' His regret was tinged with amusement, and she smiled,

'I'm sorry about you having to sleep on the floor.' For a moment she thought he was going to argue, or try to persuade. He put out a hand as though he would draw her down once more beside him, then he let the hand drop and said, 'Those were the terms, weren't they?'

'Sorry,' she said again, and then he grinned,

'So long as you don't expect me to doss down outside again.'

The rain had stopped some time during the last hour or so, but the ground would be soaking and of course she didn't. She said goodnight, promised to take her turn cooking the breakfast in the morning, and retired behind Aunt Dolly's thick dark green curtain. Just enough lamplight filtered in at the top for her to get undressed by, and she made a neat pile of her clothes at the foot of the bunk and squirmed under the sheets.

On the other side of the curtain she could hear Daniel moving around for a while, then the lamp went out and there was silence.

It had to be cooler after all that rain, but it was getting pretty humid in this little enclosed space and she crawled across the bunk to try to open the window. She had known it was stuck, she should have done this before, but she wasn't calling out in the dark and she didn't want Daniel asking her what she was doing either. So she couldn't bang the window, she could only try silent pressure, and that didn't budge it.

She put her forehead against the pane of glass, which was quite refreshing. If she should wake sweltering she would have to cool off like this, presumably the glass would stay cold. She rested a cheek against it and looked out into the dark world and the dark skies.

The hill with the Stones was up there, and although she couldn't see a thing a chill like a breeze ran over her. Beastly things! She had always hated them. When they were children they used to call them the Rollins' Stones, but the nickname hadn't made them any less awesome for Lucy. To her they were always the Dancers, always moving unseen, and now she was sleeping in their shadow, in a tiny compartment like a padded coffin.

A fine place to choose for the night, she thought. If I don't get nightmares I'll be very surprised.

She did, of course. The Stones came for her. She was up there, standing in the middle of them, a burning sun beating down on her, and they were closing in. She was suffocating in terror. They were grey and formless and utterly malevolent and she couldn't breathe or move, and they were going to roll over her like some monstrous juggernaut and she would never be able to breathe or move again.

She was trying to scream when she woke, but her throat was so dry that no sound was coming out. The effort woke her, and she seemed to be sweating from every pore. She huddled, shaking, the taste of terror still in her mouth, then she sat up groggily and pushed down the bedclothes.

She needed air, an open window or an open door, and she dragged the curtain aside and almost fell off the bunk and began to make her way down the middle of the waggon.

The huddle that was Daniel was in his sleeping bag at the far end, and she saw him start to get up. She started to say, 'It's all right.' She did say that, but she didn't get time to say, 'I'm stifling in there, I need some air,' because suddenly the space between them had gone and she was in his arms.

CHAPTER SIX

It was none of it Lucy's fault. She didn't have a chance to say any more before Daniel kissed her cheek, the corner of her mouth. His breath was warm and his hands were cool and expert, sliding the nightdress from her shoulders, holding her close against his hard lean body; and suddenly she was responding as hungrily as though she had been starved all her life, her fingers digging into his shoulder blades, lips parting as he kissed her openly and deeply. She was weak with longing from head to foot, cleaving to him, longing for him.

'Lucy,' her name was in a husky voice she hardly recognised, and he was lifting her, carrying her, and if he hadn't said a word she would have kept her arms clasped around his neck and let him carry let to the warm soft bunk.

Lucy . . . Celia . . . Was this how it had happened with Celia? The same madness, the alchemy of sex. 'No!' she sobbed. And although he still held her he stood still, and she writhed frantically away from him until he let her stand upright, the floor of the waggon beneath her bare feet.

'No!' she said again, her voice rising like the wail of a child. Daniel's skin looked shining white in the darkness, his hair black and his eyes dark as the night, and she felt the terror of the nightmare again. She was shaking with fear, babbling for her life, it seemed. 'There's no air in there. I woke up choking. I can't open the window and I had the most hellish nightmare—the Dancers, the Stones, were all around me. They were coming for me.'

She backed to the door and pulled down the bolt and swung the top window wide, and a wave of cold night air washed over her, making her gasp and cringe.

'If you're thinking of going out,' said Daniel conversationally, 'mind the plates.'

Lucy had been in two minds whether to run for it. She had thought that she had gone too far, let too much happen, to cry 'Stop', and she could hardly believe she was hearing this cool amused quip.

She looked back and Daniel was walking towards the bunk at the far end of the waggon. She saw head and shoulders outlined against the far window, then he called, 'I think somebody was over-liberal with the paint. Get me a knife.'

She twitched her nightdress over the shoulder that was bared, and picked up one of the knives they had used for supper. It was in a plastic bucket on the unlit stove, waiting for morning. She rubbed it clean on a tea towel. 'Can you see what you're doing?' Her voice was still unsteady. 'Shall I get the matches?'

She could have set fire to the place with a lighted match, the way her hands were shaking, and she certainly daren't touch the lamp, but he said, 'It's all right. Just give me a knife.'

She stretched across the bunk to give it to him, and pulled the curtain right back, then watched as he worked the knife up and down between the window frame and the surround, alternating with the occasional banged fist on the unyielding wood.

The atmosphere was rapidly chilling and she picked up her cotton skirt, from her pile of clothes at the bottom of the bunk, and wrapped it round her like a shawl. Daniel was only wearing briefs, kneeling on the bunk, working on the window. 'Shall I get you something to put on your shoulders?' she asked.

Her eyes were accustomed to the dark now, she could see quite clearly, but her mind wasn't too clear. 'You might shut the door,' he suggested, and she stammered, 'Gosh, yes, it is getting cold, isn't it?' She stepped over the sleeping bag and shut the door; she hardly knew what she was doing. She went back down the waggon again and Daniel thumped once more all around the window frame, grunting,

'It won't bloody budge. I suppose I ought to be hacking away outside. Have you ever had this window open?'

'I don't remember. I don't think so.'

'No, and I'll tell you we're not going to have it open tonight.' He got off the bunk. 'So you'd better leave the curtain open and then you're less likely to get the Dancers after you.'

'Yes.' She clutched her improvised shawl around her. 'I'm sorry,' she said miserably.

'So am I.' But he smiled. 'I thought you were making that first move you talked about.'

'I might have known I was going to be asphyxiated behind this lot. It's like an iron curtain.'

'Your aunt Dolly belongs to the better-death-than-dishonour generation.'

He could smile, but it would have been terrible if she had let him seduce her, as he had Celia, and she had been so close to it. The weakness was still in her. Her legs were like jelly. She wanted to sink down on the bunk and let him take her in his arms again, and love her with laughter and tenderness and passion.

She said, 'Please don't——' although he was doing nothing, except standing there, smiling at her.

'Don't worry.' He cupped her chin, and her face tightened and he kissed her closed eyes. 'Unless the lady's willing the game's not worth the candle.'

Of course it was a game to him. She said, 'Well, the lady isn't.'

'So goodnight, Lucy.'

He walked to the sleeping bag and got into it, and she climbed back on to the bunk. She mustn't say any more tonight. Not another word.

It took her a long time to fall asleep. She didn't think she would sleep at all because she was a mass of quiver-

ing nerve ends. It was the nightmare, of course, running
into the first arms to be consoled. But the way she had
clung to Daniel hadn't been for simple reassurance. It
had been a surge of passion like nothing she had ever
known before. She could have forgotten everything,
and woken lacerated with regret.

She did fall asleep at last, and woke feeling ashamed
of herself but knowing that it could have been much
worse. She remembered right away. The curtain was
open, and the sleeping bag was on the settee; there was
no sign of Daniel.

The dawn chorus was in full throat. She must have
slept heavily, her head burrowed into the pillow, or
the birds would have disturbed her before now. She
lay, listening to the shrill twittering of the starlings
and the hoarse throb of a wood pigeon, giving thanks
for the little miracle that had her waking alone in this
bed this morning.

It was no thanks to her. She could have made an
irredeemable mistake last night and a complete fool
of herself. She dressed quickly. It wasn't raining outside, but it wasn't the morning for alfresco meals, the
cooking and eating would have to be done in the
waggon, so she pulled out the table again and started
to prepare breakfast.

Daniel must be taking a walk. He could have gone
over to the barn to fetch William, or walked down
into the village to buy a newspaper. Or he could be
climbing the hill for another look at the Dancers. Perhaps he wasn't too happy about facing her this morning. It might be embarrassing. It had been a torrid
couple of minutes, and then a shrieking rejection. Her
plan had been to reject him, so that he decided he was
wasting his time with Lucy Friis, but she had meant
to do it coolly, not gibbering like an idiot. And now,
in the clear morning light, she wasn't too happy about
facing Daniel either.

She owed him some sort of explanation, but she

couldn't really explain it herself. She knew why she had said, 'No,' but it wasn't so easy to explain why she had nearly said nothing at all, just clung to him.

She saw him coming across the field, and she poured boiling water on the instant coffee and put the frying pan on the Calor stove. She could feel her face starting to colour, and a guilty blush was all she needed to feel really naïve. If she kept well back in the shadows perhaps he wouldn't notice her flaring cheeks.

'Hello,' she said brightly. 'What's it like out there?'

'Not bad at all.'

'Have you been for a walk? I thought you might be buying a newspaper.'

'Why should we want a newspaper?' He grinned cheerfully at her. One thing he was not was embarrassed. He looked as though nothing had happened to alter anything, and Lucy said inanely,

'Well, for the news.'

'I can do without that.'

'You're not bothered about the state of the world?'

'What do you think?'

She thought that he wasn't, that his only concern was for himself, and it was probably part of his charm, the selfish easy way he moved through life, taking nothing to heart. He said, 'I did wash the plates.'

'What?'

'The rain worked, but I thought you'd be happier if they got the bucket treatment.'

'Oh!' She had laid the table with clean plates and cutlery, she hadn't wondered how they got clean—she had had other things to think about. 'I forgot you put them outside,' she said.

'You haven't got much of a memory, have you?' Daniel seated himself on the settee and pulled one of the coffee mugs closer, and she concentrated on frying the bacon with her back towards him.

Something else I'd like to forget,' she said. 'Last night.'

'Why not?'

'I'm sorry.'

'Sorry about what? The yes or the no?' He was treating it as a joke but she wanted to put the record straight.

'About the yes,' she said. 'I was half asleep and I reacted—well, oddly.'

'I wouldn't say that. Your first reaction seemed——'

'Natural?' She snapped out the word. 'Well, I think it was odd, and I'm trying to explain that I was half asleep and I didn't really know——'

'Ah, I see.' She turned to hear what he saw, because he sounded as though he had hit on the reason. 'You didn't know it was me. Now who did you think it was?'

This was even more of a joke. His smile was brilliant and mocking and she thought—if he knew the full story he wouldn't keep quiet. He'd tell it around. He'd think it was the funniest thing.

'None of your business,' she said. 'But thanks anyway, because I did ask for trouble and it would probably have served me right if you hadn't let me go.'

'No danger,' he said lightly. He drank some coffee, while she tried to decide if she was relieved or insulted. A little of both, she supposed. He went on, 'You gave me fair warning that you'd scream "Rape" if I held on to you against your will, and sound carries in the countryside. And country folk probably turn out quicker, when somebody starts yelling blue murder, than your average city dweller. And with pitchforks.'

'Very comical!' she muttered.

'Mind you,' Daniel sounded as though he was beginning to enjoy the scenario he was creating, 'I'd like to have heard you explaining to your rescuers what you were doing in the waggon, with an all but naked man, if you didn't want a hand laid on you. Aboard the lugger, so to speak.'

The bacon spat a pinpoint of hot fat at her, and she cried 'Ouch!' and put her wrist to her mouth. 'You finish cooking this,' she said crossly, moving out of splash range. 'I don't want any. I want to get home. I came because it's my waggon and if anybody was taking it on the open road I wanted to come along. I came for the ride, not the sex, and I've apologised if it was my fault things nearly got out of hand last night——'

'Not a bit of it,' said Daniel cheerfully. 'The point of no return was nowhere near reached.'

That was a snub for her, telling her she hadn't stirred him unduly, but she had. He had been as desperate for her as she had been for him—she had been held so close she had to know—and yet he had let her go. Her breakaway had been a panic flight, but his had been such self-control that there was something almost inhuman about it.

She went to the bunk and began to pack her nightdress and housecoat in the little case, and Daniel said, 'Don't be silly. Come and eat your breakfast.'

'I don't want——' But he was right, she was behaving childishly, and she shut the lid of the case and came back to the table. 'All right,' she said, 'but I would like to get back as soon as possible. I don't know about you, but I've had about enough of this little jaunt.'

William took them home, and Daniel took the reins most of the way, although it was Lucy who brought the waggon through Moreton Meadows high street and down the road to the shop. Aunt Dolly saw the colourful vardo passing the window and rushed to the door to reassure herself that Lucy, sitting up there beside Daniel, looked healthy and happy.

Lucy waved, 'Hi!'

'Everything go all right?' Aunt Dolly called.

'Of course,' Lucy called back, and Daniel jumped down to guide William through the archway into the yard. Aunt Dolly trotted along beside them demanding,

'Did you take good care of her?'

'As good as she'd let me,' said Daniel. 'Whoa there, feller!'

There was a bustle of activity, getting the waggon on to the lawn and William from between the shafts. Uncle Joe had emerged from the workshed, and Aunt Dolly went back into the shop, to slip on the latch and hurry out again, and between them they managed it.

William's owners would be collecting him later. He would be waiting for them in a little paddock about five minutes away, so Lucy and Daniel took him along.

It had been a quiet journey home. Lucy hadn't been able to think of much to say, and when she did come up with something it had always sounded stilted. Daniel had seemed content enough, jogging along. When he spoke to her she answered, of course, but for the life of her she couldn't show any animation.

She just wanted to get back and put on her working clothes and do some work. A few hours in the workshed might help. There was some order and some sense in the patterns and pictures she painted, but this business of Celia and Daniel was nothing but a depressing mixed-up mess.

As they walked William down the road, and into the lane where the paddock was, she went over what she had to say to Daniel. She could have said it without travelling over half Gloucestershire in a gipsy waggon with him, because by now her smart idea, of dealing his pride a blow that would keep him away from Lucy Friis for ever, had gone up in a puff of smoke. It was her own ego that had taken the knocks. She would remember for a long time how near she had been to abandoning every restraint, and she was the one who had thought she could always play it cool.

'Oh, you are a clever girl,' Celia had said, when Lucy promised her that everything was going to be all right. But Lucy hadn't been very clever in the last few days. The whole idea had been daft from the start.

They closed the five-barred gate behind them, and took William well into the paddock before removing his bridle and leading rein. Daniel stroked his nose,

and got a head nuzzling his shoulder in return—
William's affectionate goodbye.

'I enjoyed our trip,' said Daniel, to William and to
Lucy. 'We must do it again.'

'It was fun,' she said, and some of it was, but not all
by any means. Some of it had been dreadful.

'Can I see you tonight?' Daniel asked. He was turning
to walk back to the gate, but when she began,

'I've got to talk to you—' he stopped, eyebrows raised. There had been plenty of time for talking since Sunday night, and she had sat beside him all morning hardly
uttering a word. He must be wondering what this was
about and she tried to say it all as quickly as possible. 'I
don't want to see you again. It's been interesting,
meeting again like this but I would rather say goodbye
now. If you don't mind.'

She expected him to say, 'But I do mind,' and to demand, 'Why?'

'I'm busy,' she muttered, 'I don't have time—'

'That's all right,' he cut in. 'I won't get in the way of
work.'

They were standing in the middle of the paddock, facing each other, with William's great head looming over
them as though he was some sort of referee, and Lucy
said through clenched teeth, 'Look, Cyprus was a
mistake. I don't want to remember what happened in
Cyprus.'

'So I've gathered,' said Daniel drily. 'All right, we'll
forget it. Never a mention of Cyprus.'

But he wasn't being sent away easily and she was getting desperate. 'Can't you understand English? I don't
want to see you again.'

'Tell me what I've done.' He sounded as though he
cared, and he probably thought she was piqued because
he hadn't persisted last night. 'Come on,' he was starting to smile at her now. 'Nobody can have too many
friends.'

'You want to be my friend?' She didn't believe that,

she couldn't see him settling for platonic arrangements, and when he laughed and said,

'That as well,' she snapped,

'When are you going home?' and started for the gate, as though if she left him behind that would be the end of it.

'That depends,' he said, striding beside her while she took two quick paces to his one slow one.

'Depends on what?' If he said, 'On you,' what was she going to do, except tell him to get lost in even stronger terms? She had wanted him to go quietly but that hope was receding all the time.

He opened the gate for her, following her through. The path was just wide enough for two abreast, and she walked in the middle of it so that he shouldn't take her arm. Behind her he said, 'I'm not just on holiday here. I'd come down to look over a cottage.'

Lucy felt herself sway briefly, croaking, 'What for?'

'I'm buying it.'

She stood stock still, her heart thudding, and a little group of people swirled round her, and Daniel came level with her, telling her, 'I'll be an absentee neighbour most of the time, but I've been looking for a small house or cottage for quite a while. It narrowed down to either here or Cornwall, and this is more convenient.'

Why couldn't it have been Cornwall? Celia would go crazy. 'Where exactly?' asked Lucy.

'Lower Meon.' That was only a few miles away, and she couldn't even begin to think what they were going to do now. She said,

'You kept very quiet about it.'

He shrugged. 'I'd have shown you the house today, but you weren't in a mood for sightseeing.'

They had passed a signpost pointing to Lower Meon and Daniel had said, 'It has a Norman church and I'd like you to see——' and she'd said, 'I've seen it, and practically every other village in the Cotswolds has got its own little cathedral. Haven't you noticed?' The village would have taken them slightly out of their way and she was anxious to get home.

She walked on now. This had changed everything. If Daniel was going to be living in these parts he was almost bound to come across Celia, sooner or later, and Celia would have to be prepared for that. At the shop door Lucy said huskily, 'I do have work to do.'

'You told me.' He ran a finger down her face. 'I'll keep in touch,' and then he had gone, striding away, getting a second look from more than one woman. Lucy watched their heads swinging round, and sighed as she pushed open the shop door.

Aunt Dolly greeted her with, 'He came for the table about an hour ago. The birthday present. Very pleased with it, he was.'

'I'm glad,' said Lucy. 'I'll just get out of these clothes and then I'll start on some work. The waggon can wait, can't it?'

The shop was empty and Aunt Dolly followed her to the connecting door asking, 'Did you go the way your Uncle Joe wrote out for you?'

'Yes. We had a cup of tea with the Thornetts. Mrs Thornett asked to be remembered to you. Coll and Sandra are still at home.'

'We didn't expect you back until tonight.' Lucy knew that she was looking strained, she had just had a nasty shock, she felt grey with anxiety, and Aunt Dolly wanted to know why. You could almost see the questions trembling on her lips. 'You don't look much better for the break,' Aunt Dolly decided.

'Oh, it was all right.'

'And what about this young man?'

'He was all right too.'

'I hope he behaved himself,' said Aunt Dolly severely, and Lucy's mouth quivered although she didn't feel much like laughing.

'Of course he behaved,' she said. 'He was nicely

brought up. He told me himself.' She didn't say anything about the cottage, but she left Aunt Dolly wondering if her misgivings about them going off on their
own like that had been justified.

Lucy did tell Uncle Joe. She had been in the workshed the best part of an hour, sketching out a design of
wheat and poppies on the back of a kitchen dresser,
and Uncle Joe hadn't asked any questions at all. When
they'd first arrived he'd asked, 'Have a good time?' and
they'd both said yes, they had. But since Lucy came into
the workshed, and started work, he hadn't said a word
about Daniel, nor about the trip.

That was significant because, although Uncle Joe
was a man of few words, he usually enjoyed a joke
about Lucy's boy-friends. It was as though he suspected that this was no ordinary happy-go-lucky dating,
but something that she didn't want to talk about.

He was reminding her that there was a sale tomorrow, in an old manor house in one of the villages,
when she said suddenly, 'Daniel's buying a cottage in
Lower Meon. He's coming down here to live.'

Joe Partridge's hands stilled and he looked up from
his work. 'When did he decide on that?'

'It's nothing to do with me,' Lucy said wearily. 'He'd
decided before he even remembered I live here.'

Uncle Joe looked straight at her. 'You don't seem
very happy about it,' and she couldn't meet his eyes
because she wanted to tell him the whole story, and if
she did he would say she should never have got involved. Perhaps she shouldn't, she hadn't exactly
helped matters. He could well get straight on to the
telephone to order Celia to make a clean breast of it
to Howard. His reaction would be to protect Lucy, not
Celia. He had no time for hypocrisy, and now that she
was in so deep it was too late for Lucy to ask for his
advice.

She said, 'I was an idiot to go off in that waggon,' and
as Uncle Joe's wiry grey eyebrows came together in a

scowl she grinned wryly, 'It's all right, Aunt Dolly asked me if he "behaved" himself. She meant did he keep to his own end of the waggon after lights out, and he did. But I was glad to get back. He isn't my sort.'

'Then will you take a bit of advice?' said Uncle Joe.

'What?'

'If you've made up your mind you don't want any more to do with him you stick to that. Tell him straight, and don't play him around.' Joe Partridge went back to the inlay of veneer he was meticulously repairing on the top of a Victorian sewing box, 'Because there's something about that young man,' he said, 'I can't rightly say what, but I wouldn't want you to be making an enemy of him.'

'Neither would I,' said Lucy, and she knew that Uncle Joe had sensed what she had felt, that Daniel Stewart could be a heartless and dangerous man.

She stayed in the workshed until the shop closed and Aunt Dolly was badgering her to come and have some supper, and then she said, 'Thanks, love, but I think I should be getting home, and I've still got the waggon to empty.'

'That won't take long,' said Aunt Dolly promptly. 'And how do you know your mother will have a meal waiting for you?'

Lucy didn't, but there would be food in the house, she could soon get herself something, and she didn't think she could face Aunt Dolly asking questions the whole meal long.

'You come and have something to eat,' Aunt Dolly ordered. 'Joe, you tell her. She's looking peaky.'

For a gentle lady Aunt Dolly was almost impossible to resist, and Lucy was too dejected to put up much fight. So she sighed and said, 'Okay, I'll be along,' and put away her tools, took off her smock, and went up to the cottage bathroom to wash her hands.

The meal was waiting when she came down into the

kitchen, Aunt Dolly's rabbit pie, and she made herself eat. She was more depressed than she had been at any time since Celia told her about meeting Daniel, because for the first time she felt quite helpless. Daniel was not going away. He could be a shadow over all the years ahead, and if it wasn't this week or next some time he was bound to realise that it had been Celia and not Lucy in Cyprus. Or, what was just as likely, Celia would crack up, with an aftermath of bitter unhappiness for them all.

Uncle Joe brought the catalogue of tomorrow's sale to the table with him, and went very slowly through it, item by item. Lucy knew why and loved him for it, and said, 'Yes, all right,' when he scribbled figures in the margins. There was no need for this, but it was business talk and it kept Aunt Dolly off Daniel.

She did say, when they'd finished a fresh fruit salad and were sitting with a cup of tea, 'I've always said you've got to live with somebody to know them,' and Uncle Joe and Lucy blinked at her. 'Well,' said Aunt Dolly, 'it's plain enough that you two got on each other's nerves.'

'Hang on,' said Lucy, 'a couple of days' holiday isn't living together, but no, I reckon we didn't rub along too smoothly.'

She must phone Celia and prepare her. She couldn't advise her, but in the circumstances Celia might decide she had no alternative, she had to tell Howard, and he was the last man to have any sympathy with that kind of confession. Lucy could imagine the scene that would follow, and she felt sick.

Aunt Dolly was saying something, a murmur of words that Lucy didn't hear clearly because she was listening to the terrible words in her head that Howard was saying to Celia. She shivered and tried to blot out the picture and the sounds, then she saw Aunt Dolly's worried face and said, 'Sorry, what did you say?'

'I said there's no need to look like that. It isn't the

end of the world.' Aunt Dolly topped up Lucy's nearly empty teacup, and Lucy forced a smile although the bleak thought pierced her that Celia's happy protected little world might well be coming to an end ...

She saw the car standing outside the house as her van turned the corner of the road. There were often cars parked outside, Maman had plenty of friends and so did Lucy, but this car was not only unfamiliar but spectacular. It was a steel grey Scimitar, elegant and expensive; it immediately brought Daniel to mind, it looked his kind of car.

She didn't know that, of course. She had been thinking of Daniel before she saw it, he had been at the forefront of her mind for hours now, and if there had been a taxi or a bicycle outside her home she would still have wondered if that could have brought him here.

She turned into the short drive, opened the garage door and drove into the garage. But when she turned off the ignition tiredness struck her, so that she let her hands fall into her lap and slumped back in her seat. She suddenly felt too weary to move, and that was because she didn't want to go into the house, because she was convinced that Daniel would be waiting there.

He wouldn't even have to enquire to find out her address, it was the only Friis in the phone book. He could come along and introduce himself to Maman, tell her where he had met Lucy, and Maman would be the first to know, after Lucy, that the only time in all their married life that Howard had let Celia go away alone she had picked up a devastatingly attractive man and told him a pack of lies.

Oh God, poor Maman! And poor Lucy. She felt hollow and jerky as a wound-up toy, sitting in her car in the little shadowy garage. She was almost past caring. She couldn't do any more. It was like being in a dark maze with high hedges all around. If Daniel had driven a bulldozer through the hedges at least she could get out. It would be destructive and terrible, but she wouldn't have to twist and turn any longer.

She fumbled with her key in the door, steeling herself to step into the hall, and when she did the first thing she heard was laughter. Maman sounded as though she was having the time of her life, so it was unlikely that her visitor was Daniel. Unless he had only just arrived and so far Cyprus hadn't been mentioned.

Lucy supposed she was relieved. Of course it was better than finding Maman in a state of shock, but these razor's-edge escapes were playing havoc with Lucy's nerves. She was wrung out now, and when she opened the drawing room door and it *was* Daniel, sitting in an armchair with a drink on a table beside him, she could have picked up the glass and emptied it over his head.

He stood up, looking pleased to see her, and she said dourly, 'I thought I told you I was busy tonight.'

'*Lucy!*' her mother chided her. 'Daniel and I have been getting to know each other.' She smiled at him, and of course he did seem just the kind of man that Maman would approve of, with his aristocratic good looks and inborn self-confidence. If she got any idea that he might be successful as well she would certainly decide that he was her ideal second son-in-law.

'Has he told you he's in the photography trade?' asked Lucy. 'And he doesn't make all that much money. Do you?'

'I'm no millionaire,' he agreed, as Maman wafted such mercenary thoughts aside.

'Daniel was telling me,' she said, 'that I have one of the most photogenic faces he has ever seen.' Her features were good, she was still a very attractive woman, but that was nonsense. He was winning her round, and it seemed to Lucy such an obvious ploy that she almost burst into derisive laughter. 'He is going to take some pictures of me,' said Maman.

'That *will* be nice,' said Lucy.

'It will be my pleasure,' Daniel said gravely.

'Don't bank on it,' said Lucy.

'Of course,' said Maman, 'Celia is always having her photograph taken.' There were photographs on the wall, on the mantelshelf, a wedding picture stood on the table beside Daniel's glass of whisky. He must have seen them all and Lucy knew that Maman would have been talking about Celia, because she always did.

She was angry that he had come to this house, it was an intrusion. He had been an intruder from the beginning and she sat fuming, because she couldn't turn him out while Maman was practically flirting with him, all her Gallic coquetry responding to his flattering charm.

Lucy sat down, declining a drink, taking hardly any part in the conversation. Perhaps if it had looked like moving into risky channels she would have tried to steer it out, but she was fed up with the whole thing. It was ridiculous that she couldn't break loose from somebody who was bedevilling her. If it hadn't been for Celia she would have walked out of this room as soon as she saw him sitting here. As it was she stayed, and felt chained to her chair, because she was afraid to go and leave him with Maman.

They didn't seem to notice her ill humour. Daniel was name-dropping, and Maman loved that. As a photographer it was just possible that he had met some of the famous folk he was talking about. Maman liked stories about the rich and famous, and kept saying that he must meet Celia and Howard, and Lucy sat grim-faced. Although in any other circumstances she would have been giggling, because most of the time he was very funny indeed. Maman laughed at his stories, and tried to persuade him to have another whisky, then sent Lucy to make the coffee, and generally carried on as though he was a favourite guest.

She was intrigued about the house he was buying. She thought she knew it. When he explained its exact location she said, 'Oh yes, behind the high laurel hedge. A most delightful little home.'

'You must come and look it over,' said Daniel. 'What are you doing tomorrow?' He was asking Lucy that too, and while Maman was gurgling that she would be delighted Lucy was saying that there was an auction and she would have no time at all to spare.

Maman frowned at her and suggested, 'The day after tomorrow?'

'I'll leave you a key,' said Daniel. 'But after tomorrow I shall be away until the weekend.' He gave Maman one of his sweetest smiles. 'I do hope you like it,' he said, as though if she didn't he might well call the deal off, and Lucy yawned, making a production of it.

'How inconsiderate of me!' Daniel stood up, sounding contrite. 'You're tired and I'm sitting around here, keeping you from your bed.'

It wasn't half past nine yet, his eyes were laughing at her, but of course she wanted him to go, and before Maman could protest Lucy was on her feet too, saying, 'Goodnight, then,' and holding the door open for him.

'Lucy!' Maman shrieked at her, but Daniel said goodnight to Maman, thanked her for her hospitality and said he would pick her up in the morning, about half past eleven if that was convenient, to take her over to inspect the house in which he planned to live.

By the time they'd spent another hour or two together the cat would surely be out of the bag, but Lucy had given up. She couldn't stop what was coming, and she went to the front door with Daniel and opened it for him stony-faced.

'Do you mind me taking your mother round the house?' he asked.

'Why should I? She'll enjoy it, so long as it's a desirable residence in a good neighbourhood. She wouldn't give a two-up-two-down a second look.'

Maman's snobbery had always been rather endearing. Lucy and her father had smiled at it, and it was often a joke to Uncle Joe and Aunt Dolly too. But the cornerstone of her pride was Celia's marriage, and God only knew what lay ahead for that.

Lucy didn't want Daniel to come near her. She backed against the wall, moving away from him so that he had to get her message, and he hesitated for a moment. Then he said, 'Let's hope we live up to her expectations,' and she wondered if he was smiling as he walked out to his car.

Lucy wasn't. She could have wept. She shut the door but stayed in the hall until she heard the car start up and drive away, and for a little longer. Maman came through with the coffee cups and asked, 'What are you doing there?'

'Nothing.'

'I do not understand you.' It wasn't the first time Maman had said that, but she didn't usually add, 'It isn't like you.' She went into the kitchen, putting the tray down on the table with a bump that made the coffee cups jump. 'You do not sulk,' she said. 'You have never been a sullen girl, so why did you sit there looking so cross and hardly saying a civil word?'

'He shouldn't have come here,' said Lucy. 'I told him I couldn't see him tonight. That meant I didn't want to.'

'But why not? He is such a charming man.' Maman's face was alight with enthusiasm. 'So amusing, so handsome. And not married.'

'You asked him that, of course?'

'But of course,' said Maman archly.

Lucy went to the sink and started the washing up. 'Did he also tell you that he doesn't reckon on marriage? Not for him.'

'All men say that.' Maman made a wise face, and Lucy said.

'They don't, you know. And this one means it.' When her mother laughed she turned from the bowl of suds and reached for a cloth to dry her hands. 'Do I lie to you?' she asked.

'No.'

This was another Lucy her mother hadn't seen before, a white-faced girl with haggard eyes. 'Don't get any ideas about Daniel,' said Lucy. 'Just believe me when I say that I have very good reason for not wanting to see him.'

'But—' Maman began, 'what—?' Her mind darted among dark explanations and cringed away from them. But Lucy's steady burning gaze frightened her.

'I don't want you to go looking around that house of his tomorrow,' said Lucy. 'And I don't want him coming here.'

'But he will come. You heard him say.'

'I'll phone the hotel and tell him you had to go out.'

'If you say so.' Maman looked suddenly lost and afraid, and Lucy put an arm around her.

'It's all right, love,' she said. 'It's just one of those things.' As she spoke she knew how hollow her reassurance was. She said, 'Come on, I will have that drink. Leave the cups,' and she took Maman back into the drawing room, and poured out a small Campari for herself and a dry sherry for Maman, and tried to make her smile again, suggesting they might take a holiday together in a month or two. In the off season they could go abroad quite reasonably, and Lucy painted glowing pictures, and Maman agreed that an autumn break might be nice and began to reminisce about Paris.

They sat discussing the possibilities for about half an hour, then Lucy said, 'I've got a letter to post, I think I'll walk round with it. Shall I turn the television on for you?' Maman consulted the newspaper, selected her programme, and seemed to settle down comfortably, and Lucy ran all the way to the little village post office.

The phone box outside was empty, which was lucky. She couldn't have hung around, while somebody got through an interminable conversation, without Maman getting worried, and she was anxious to ring Celia. She would have had to wait for Maman to go to bed before she could have risked calling her from home, and that might be any time. Besides, if she got Celia out of bed Howard was going to ask what the excitement was about, but around ten o'clock it was natural enough that Lucy should be calling her sister.

Celia answered, with only the faintest quickening of anxiety in her voice when she asked, 'How are you? How are things?'

'Is Howard there? Can you talk?'

'He's still at the House. It looks like being another late sitting.' Nanny would be around, but Lucy said,

'Well, the news isn't too good.'

'You mean he's guessed? You didn't tell him?' Celia had to be alone to say that, and Lucy went on quickly,

'No. But he wasn't just on holiday down here, he was buying a cottage in Lower Meon. He's going to be around.'

'Around where?'

'Around *here*, for goodness' sake!' Lucy sounded the more jittery of the two. 'If he's living here,' she pointed out, 'you're probably going to meet him sooner or later, so I'm just warning you.'

'You've seen him again, then?' Celia sounded almost her calm placid self, and Lucy suspected that she was feeling safe and far away from it all in the London flat. At any rate she was no longer carrying on as though she had been hit by a bolt from the blue.

'Of course I've seen him,' said Lucy. 'That's how I know about the cottage.'

'So you didn't take my advice?' The advice on the tape, about avoiding Daniel. Lucy had thought she had a better plan, but it hadn't come off. She said,

'He isn't easy to get rid of.'

'I expect he fancies you,' said Celia. 'Most men do.'

Lucy's nerves were twanging like guitar strings, but Celia hardly sounded worried at all. She had been nearly out of her mind before she went away, but now she sounded as though she was smiling.

'Have you told Howard?' Lucy asked.

'Not yet, but I suppose I'd better. What I thought I might do was tell him that Daniel's turned up again, and that we met in Cyprus but I said I was you.'

'And what's your excuse for using my name?' snapped Lucy.

'Because I didn't want to talk politics. Once you admit you're an M.P.'s wife all anybody wants to talk is politics.'

Not a man who's trying to chat you up, Lucy thought, sickeningly sure that Howard was not going to swallow this. 'And you've been playing it along as a joke since,' Celia went on. 'Well, you do have a crazy sense of humour, don't you? Howard knows that.'

Howard would have to think she was crazy all through to imagine she was getting laughs out of this, and she remembered Celia saying, 'It's no joke, it isn't funny.'

'What else are you going to tell him?' she asked wearily.

'Nothing,' said Celia.

'What if Daniel talks?'

'He couldn't prove it; and he isn't really likely to run around telling folk that he slept with me, is he?'

It didn't sound like Celia talking, and Lucy looked out into the empty street and tears blurred her eyes so that everything seemed unfamiliar and strange. She said, 'I don't know what he's likely to do. I don't know what anybody's likely to do any more.'

'I might as well come back at the weekend,' said Celia. 'Howard's coming back, he's got a meeting or something. I was going to stay on with the children for the fortnight, but if Daniel isn't on holiday there's not much point in me not coming home, is there?'

'Not a lot,' Lucy agreed.

In the next few days she told herself countless times that Celia had to know Howard better than she did. Perhaps Celia could tell him about meeting Daniel and pretending to be Lucy, and make it sound harmless, but Lucy doubted it. Howard Clendinnen was no fool. He was going to ask questions, and before he was through he was going to get answers.

They were bad days for Lucy. She had phoned Daniel and told him that her mother couldn't get over to see the house. He hadn't seemed surprised, nor had he mentioned seeing Lucy again.

She rang Celia twice. Once Celia had other folk around, but she sounded normal and cheerful. On the Friday night both Celia and Howard had gone out to dinner, and Nanny said they would all be home tomorrow and they had had a lovely little holiday. She put Melanie on to say hello, and neither Nanny nor Melanie sounded as though the atmosphere of the household had changed in any way.

Perhaps it wasn't going to. Perhaps they would see no more of Daniel. if they didn't then Howard might accept that he was one of those holiday bores to whom you'd give any name but your own. Of course, if Howard ever should meet Daniel he's realise that no married woman would pose as unattached, to a man that sexily good-looking, unless she was looking for trouble.

Perhaps they wouldn't meet, but Lucy worried and fretted even while she was working, and lay awake worrying at night. By Saturday she had probably lost several pounds in weight, if she had bothered to weigh herself.

Saturday was market day and Lucy was kept busy, but that didn't stop her remembering that Celia and Howard were due back, wondering whether she should go round, whether she should phone, wondering, worrying . . .

She arrived home just after six o'clock. The television was on in the drawing room, but Maman was sitting, holding Celia's wedding photograph, looking at it. She hadn't heard Lucy's car, nor Lucy coming into the house, and Lucy thought—she knows!

Her sudden movement in the doorway caught her mother's eye, and Maman turned and smiled and said, 'I hoped you wouldn't be late, I don't have a bridge party tonight, too many on holiday, but Celia phoned and we're going round there for dinner.'

Celia's housekeeper was a good cook, but Lucy wondered how much of this meal was going to be eaten, what sort of an evening lay ahead. At the moment Maman seemed pleased with life. Her eyes were shining, the way they always did when she talked of Celia and Howard. Perhaps even more than usual. She looked quite excited, biting her lip. 'Sit down, darling,' she said. 'I have something to tell you.'

She couldn't know, or she wouldn't be smiling like that. 'Daniel rang a few minutes ago,' Maman went on, and Lucy's knees gave way so that it was as well there was a chair handy. 'You haven't been happy, have you?' Maman answered herself. 'And it is Daniel, isn't it, because he doesn't believe in marriage? When you told me there were reasons why you wouldn't see him again I thought about drugs.' She hesitated, glanced away. 'And—other things. But then I knew that no one who looks as fit as Daniel does could be on drugs. That is impossible.' She looked back again, smiling. 'And certainly he is a real man, there is no doubt about that. So you had to be unhappy because you saw no future with him.'

Lucy couldn't say anything. She could only listen to Maman, becoming more confidential and more in earnest with every word. 'But I do not believe that Daniel would not choose to marry the right girl. I feel that he is disillusioned with marriage because so many marriages go wrong these days. But when I showed him Celia and Howard's wedding picture he looked at it for a long time, almost as though he was discovering something. Perhaps he was thinking of you as a bride —as his bride, perhaps. Now, just now, when he phoned and asked to speak to you I thought how it might be if we showed him a really happy marriage, a really loving family.'

Lucy could feel the protests rising in her throat. 'So,' said Maman, beaming with triumph, 'I asked him to meet us tonight, at Celia's.'

CHAPTER SEVEN

LUCY thought wildly—I shall start laughing. She could feel the laughter coming up in her throat, bitter and choking. Her only hope had been to keep Howard and Daniel apart, and now Maman had arranged a meeting for the first evening Celia and Howard were home and Daniel was back in town. Not a minute wasted. It was hysterical. It all proved that you couldn't really do anything about anything. The stars ruled, O.K.

Maman said, 'Lucy? Lucy, are you all right?' and Lucy realised that it wasn't laughter in her throat, it was more like tears. She gulped and asked,

'Does Celia know?'

'Not yet.'

'Where did Daniel call from?' If he was at an hotel there might be time to stop him going round to Howard's.

'He said he was just leaving. From London, I think.'

Lucy went into the hall and phoned the Crown, and they had no record that Mr Stewart was returning. But she left a message, in case he should turn up. Would they say that Lucy phoned and tonight was off, and ask him to ring her home in the morning?

'Sure thing, Lucy,' said Carole Whittaker obligingly. 'Going all right, is it?' She meant Lucy's affair with Daniel, and Lucy bit her lip hard.

'Fine,' she said.

Then she rang Celia. The drawing room door was closed, Maman could walk into the hall any time and if she did Lucy would have to be careful what she was saying. But when she got Celia she demanded bluntly, 'Have you told Howard?'

'Well, no,' said Celia. 'He's been so busy all week

there hasn't really been a chance. He's at a meeting now, but he'll be with us for dinner. You are coming tonight, aren't you? I asked Maman.'

'She told me. I'm home.' Lucy took a deep breath. 'I'm phoning because it seems that Daniel rang up a little while ago, and she's invited him round to your house tonight.'

In the silence that followed she could hear a clock ticking. Celia must have answered the phone on the hall table by the grandfather clock. Then Celia said in a strangled voice, 'Why did you *let* her?'

'I wasn't here.'

'Can't you stop him?'

'I don't know where he is. He's been in London since Wednesday.'

'The way things are going,' said Celia wildly, 'I wonder I didn't run into him in Regent Street. The way my luck's working.' Her voice was loud and there were bound to be other people in the house, if not in the hall.

'Pull yourself together,' said Lucy sharply. 'We'll be right over,' and she fled upstairs to strip off her working clothes and wash and make up in record time. She grabbed the first dress that came to hand, a denim, pulled a comb through her hair and dashed downstairs again, where Maman viewed her unhappily and reminded her,

'You've got much prettier things than that.'

'This will do,' said Lucy, and Maman sighed.

'You never make the best of yourself. Why can't you be more like Celia?'

As they turned into the drive of Celia's house Lucy heard her mother give a different kind of sigh, one of contentment. It always happened, that 'Aaah...!' and the house was imposing, large and solidly built, standing in lawns as smooth as green velvet against a background of tall trees.

Lucy set her down at the front door and took the

van round the back, and that habit had been going on
for a long time too, because Maman didn't think vans
looked good, standing in front of the house. Lucy's
father used to chuckle, 'The tradesmen's entrance for
us.'

Nanny and Melanie had met Maman in the hall
when Lucy came through, and Celia was leaning over
the balustrade, wearing a pale blue silk kimono.
'Auntie Lucy!' Melanie grabbed her round the legs,
'we saw——' She was about to embark on the wonders
of the past week, but Celia was calling from the top of
the stairs,

'Lucy, come on up!'

Maman asked Melanie, 'What did you see, my darling?' and Lucy said,

'I'll be along to hear all about it and give you a goodnight hug.'

Maman would love helping to put the children to
bed. Lucy went upstairs and followed Celia into her
bedroom, where she was restlessly pacing the Chinese
carpet. As Lucy closed the door Celia demanded,

'Does Daniel know?'

'No. I haven't seen him since he came to our house
on Tuesday.'

'It doesn't sound much of a tale, does it, to tell
Howard?'

'You mean pretending to be me because you didn't
want to talk politics? It certainly does not.'

Under the kimono Celia was wearing a plain white
slip. Her make-up was perfect: eyes, lips, cheeks subtly
coloured, skin smooth and flawless; and her soft fair
hair, so like Lucy's in colour and texture, was drawn
into its usual chignon.

There was a pale turquoise silk dress lying on the
counterpane of the big double bed. She put it on and
its fluid lines moulded discreetly to her figure, its
plunge neckline showing only a hint of cleavage. 'I
think we could brazen it out,' she said.

'Could we?' It seemed to be Lucy's problem now, she was in as deep as Celia, who was fastening a delicate Georgian necklet of diamonds and aquamarines around her throat. Her hands were shaking a little, she was having trouble with the fastener, and her voice could have been steadier, asking,

'Why the hell did Maman tell him to come here?'

'To see a happy marriage in action,' said Lucy bitterly, and tactlessly, because Celia went pale under her shell pink blusher, then she said defiantly,

'Well, it is a happy marriage. What do you want me to do? Go on saying I'm sorry, go on saying I was a fool? Well, you've met him now, haven't you? He's a charmer, isn't he?'

'He's sexy,' Lucy agreed.

'He made a set at me and I fell for it,' wailed Celia. 'Well, I'm human, aren't I?' She took a little box from a handbag on the floor by the bed, and shook out a couple of tiny pills, swallowing them as Lucy stared. 'And don't you start fussing—they're just something to steady my nerves. I've been taking them for ages. Don't worry, they're on prescription and they're not very strong.'

Lucy hadn't realised that Celia was needing tranquillisers, and she wondered how many she had taken lately. But a couple tonight might not be a bad idea; the calmer Celia stayed the better.

Lucy looked at her twin, who could have been modelling for a fashion magazine, then glanced wryly at her own reflection in the dressing table mirror, and there seemed to be hardly any resemblance at all. 'All right,' she said, 'I'll go on with it, but you do realise that if he mentions Cyprus we're in real lumber?'

'Of course I do.' Celia hesitated with the little box of pills in her hand, and Lucy said quickly,

'I don't care how mild those are, you've had enough.'

There was a tap on the door, Nanny had brought Rolly, pink and shining from his bath, to say good-

night, and Celia kissed him gingerly, drawing back
quickly in case he should spoil her make-up.

'Come here, Rolly-polly,' said Lucy, kissing and cud-
dling him. She went along with Nanny to tuck him up
in his nursery cot, and then along to the bathroom
where Maman was rubbing Melanie down with a big
white fluffy towel. Lucy always had fun with the
children, and listening to Melanie's description of the
Changing of the Guard helped to take her mind off
Howard and Daniel.

Melanie had crayoned a picture for her, of scarlet
stick-men with huge black fuzzy heads, mounted on
stick horses. '*Very* good,' said Lucy, sitting beside Melanie's bed. 'My, aren't the soldiers handsome?'

'And *big*,' said Melanie, making wide eyes. The bear-
skins of the Household Cavalry had impressed her.
'They were nearly giants.'

'Gosh,' said Lucy, 'you must take me some day.'

She had a sharp pang of uneasiness when she said
that, listening to Melanie's promises about 'next time',
knowing how secure the future must seem to the child.
It was like seeing a crack in the smooth walls of the
house that nobody else had spotted.

One thing was sure: there must be no more evenings
like this. Daniel must be firmly excluded from their
family circle after tonight. If only they could keep up
the charade through this one meal Lucy would avoid
him like the plague in future, and she felt so dreadful
because she was so worried.

Of course she wanted Daniel to keep out of her way.
The heartache was worry and weariness. Certainly not
because she was afraid that she might miss him, and
miss something with him that might have been marvellous.

'Aunty Lucy,' said Melanie reproachfully, 'you're
not listening to me.'

'Oh, but I am,' Lucy lied. 'I'm listening to everything
you're telling me.'

'I'm not telling you nothing.' Melly's underlip quivered. 'I'm singing you a song.'

'Of course you are,' said Lucy. 'And it's a lovely song. Please go on singing it.'

She kept a smile on her face after that, and when the singing was over kissed Melanie goodnight, and tucked her up, still smiling.

Howard came home about half past seven, and looked into the drawing room where Lucy and Celia and Maman were sitting on the long settee and Celia was telling Maman whom she had met in London. 'Ah,' he said, 'my three beautiful girls.'

He still held his briefcase tucked under his arm while he kissed them all. 'Dinner smells good,' he said.

'We've got a visitor,' Celia told him, and his face fell and she smiled. 'It's all right. It's only one of Lucy's boy-friends.'

'Serious?' Howard asked. Lucy shook her head.

'Maman invited him. He rang home when I wasn't there and she invited him over here to dinner.'

'He's coming to live round here,' said Maman, 'so he'll be one of your constituents,' Howard began to laugh.

'I can see I'll have to take you on as an agent!' He was fond of Maman. It was one of the things Lucy liked about her brother-in-law, how kind he was to Maman. She could hardly bear to look at his smiling face and think what might happen during tonight's dinner party, and she jumped up and walked across to one of the big bay windows that overlooked the drive, and Celia said, 'You'll hear him coming, there's no need to stand at the window.'

She sounded teasing, it was just the right note, and Lucy thought—We might get away with it. The pills seem to have helped, Celia's playing her part well.

But when they did hear Daniel's car she saw her sister's hand grip the arm of the sofa, and felt the tension that was running through Celia's whole body. If

Lucy had been standing nearer she would have touched her, and tried to give her some reassurance, but half the room was between them, so that all Lucy could do was smile and say, 'I'll let him in.'

The car had stopped and Daniel was out, and by the time she opened the front door he was up the steps. She hardly had time for a 'Hello' before Howard had followed her into the hall.

'Hi,' said Daniel. He looked at her face fleetingly and yet as though he missed nothing, a strange searching look. Then he tilted her chin and kissed her lips, and she told herself that every nerve was screaming in aversion because she was tingling to her toes.

Howard came smiling down the hall with an out-stretched hand. 'Good evening, I'm Howard Clen-dinnen.'

'And I'm Daniel Stewart,' said Daniel, and Lucy saw the twitch of his lips, Howard did tend to announce himself as though there was a fanfare of trumpets in the background.

He was being a very welcoming host, and Daniel was probably a pleasant surprise. Some of Lucy's friends dressed rather scruffily, Howard had looked askance at more than one, but Daniel, in grey silk shirt and beautifully cut grey suit, looked more than presentable. Like Maman, Howard was favourably impressed.

Maman gave a little cry of delight as they walked into the room. She couldn't help it. She thought that Daniel would be so suitable for Lucy, such a gentleman. She had to tell him again how lovely it was to see him.

Lucy was watching Celia, who was smiling a social smile as Howard introduced his wife. 'How do you do, Mr Stewart,' said Celia. 'I'm so glad you could come.'

He knew they were twins, so he would pick out the identical features, under their individual make-up and hair-styles, but he must realise at a glance that here were two very different girls, and Lucy was glad to see Celia so calm.

She was feeling far from calm herself. She sat down on the edge of a chair, feeling as though her smile was glued on her face, making her lips so stiff that they hurt, while Howard poured Daniel a drink and they talked about the house he was buying.

'Daniel comes from London,' Maman informed them.

'I've an apartment there,' said Daniel.

'And what's your line?' Howard asked him.

'He takes photographs,' said Lucy. 'You don't do anything else, do you? You just take photographs?'

'Daniel Stewart!' Howard put down his aperitif and sat up as though a light had dawned. 'Of course! Oh, I'm a great admirer of your work.'

Are you my foot, thought Lucy cynically. She had heard Howard telling someone how much he admired, or respected, whatever it was they did, dozens of times. It made him liked, and of course it got him votes. She said drily, 'He does mainly fashion pictures. How many women's mags do you read, Howard?' and Howard smiled, then the grandfather clock in the hall chimed eight, and Celia said,

'Shall we go in?'

The dining room looked as it always had, ever since Howard's grandfather built the house and bought the furniture. The matching oak chairs, with their mulberry red brocaded seats, stood in place around the long dark oak table. The carved sideboard carried some ornate silverware, and the paintings on the walls were of the local countryside.

Lucy had always felt very secure and safe in here, but tonight she was holding her breath half the time. Howard gave several of his favourite little speeches, that the women had all heard before, while they ate cold creamy avocado soup followed by fillet of beef en croûte.

Most of the time Howard talked to Daniel, and Lucy remembered what Daniel had said about politicians, and wondered what he was thinking while he was listening so quietly. She knew that handsome mask of a face, and she felt that any minute he was going to get bored and take over the conversation, start asking questions, stirring things.

Usually she would have been chattering away herself, but tonight she could think of nothing to say. She sat there, swallowing her food, listening to Howard, and longing for the meal to end.

She envied Celia, who was looking as though she hadn't a care in the world. Why should Lucy worry if Celia didn't? As soon as they'd finished eating she was going to plead that she had paper work to do and must go home, and with luck Daniel would offer to drive her. But if he didn't, and she had to leave him here, that was just too bad, because the strain was becoming almost unendurable. She couldn't take much more.

'How's business been this week, Lucy?' Howard asked her.

'Pretty good.' So it had, but she had had a wretched week.

'You were on a business trip, weren't you, until Tuesday?' Celia was recalling what Lucy had told her. 'Where did you go?'

'Not exactly a business trip.' Lucy stirred her pudding, looking down at the dish. 'You know the gipsy caravan? We took a trip in it through the Cotswolds. Daniel wanted to hire it and I thought I'd go along.'

'Roadworthy, is it?' Howard enquired. He didn't see anything extraordinary in Lucy and her boy-friend taking to the road together, although Maman was looking surprised. Daniel said that it was, that they had had no trouble, no hitches, and Celia's wine spilt.

She had picked up her glass awkwardly and it had tilted, sending some of the contents over the edge. She grimaced with annoyance and mopped up the small pool on the shining table with a napkin. Then she reached for the decanter to refill her glass, and Lucy wondered if she should be drinking with those pills she had taken, and if she was remembering the last time she had spilt a glass of wine and Daniel had been sitting at the next table, and they had smiled at each other and he had moved over to sit beside her.

He was looking at Celia now. They all were, watching as she poured her wine and asked them, smiling, 'Anyone else?'

Howard took the decanter from her and topped up glasses, and Lucy put a hand over hers. 'That's a very beautiful ring,' said Daniel.

He wasn't talking to Lucy, she wasn't wearing a ring, but Celia always did, as well as her wedding ring. Tonight she wore an aquamarine surrounded by diamonds, in an antique setting that matched her necklet, and she said, 'Thank you. It is rather pretty, isn't it?'

Maman began to talk about Celia's jewellery, and the piece she liked best, which was a sunburst sapphire brooch again with a matching ring. 'Celia has always had such beautiful hands,' said Maman smugly, and Lucy thought—hands! Oh, my God, *hands* ...

Their hands were different. Not in size or shape, but in Celia's long elegant nails and in the rings she wore. She wouldn't have taken her wedding ring off, and she always wore beautiful rings. Did Daniel remember 'Lucy's' hands? He must have touched them, held them, and they must have touched him.

Lucy stared down into her dish of stirred icecream and fruit and felt queasy. She knew that Daniel was looking at her, and as she turned to meet his eyes his glance fell slowly and deliberately to her hands. That could have been because he was remembering what she had said, about Maman nagging that Lucy didn't have 'lady's hands'. He could have been sharing a joke. But the quirk of his eyebrows said something else, and the slow smile was making her feel very uneasy indeed.

So—he knew. But they went on with the polite table talk, and Daniel went on being the perfect dinner guest. Later there would be a reckoning when she would have to explain and try to make him understand; but he was hardly likely to ask, in front of Howard and Maman, 'By the way, which twin was in Cyprus with me last year?'

She prayed he wouldn't, but she couldn't be absolutely sure. It was like sitting on a powder keg. The tick of the grandfather clock, through the open door into the hall, sounded like a time-bomb.

Celia hadn't realised that she had given herself away. She was a little flushed, either from the wine or the strain, but when Lucy said, 'I hate to do this, but I've a pile of paper work waiting and I shall have to be leaving you,' she saw the relief in Celia's face. Celia thought they had got away with it, and Howard said regretfully to Daniel,

'I suppose that means we're losing you too.'

'I'm afraid it does,' said Daniel.

Maman decided to stay the night. There was plenty of room for her and always a welcome, and Howard and Celia came out to the car to wave goodbye.

Lucy sat silently in the passenger seat until they were out of the drive and on to the road, waiting for Daniel to say something. Of course he knew, but she wasn't committing herself while there was the faintest chance that he might not.

Then he said, 'Why did she use your name?'

'It was the first that came into her head.'

'Interesting.' He drove smoothly and fairly fast, and Lucy watched the lights of oncoming cars and felt as though she was rushing towards the biggest smash-up of her life. But Daniel was a good driver and this was a good car, and the smash was not likely to be physical. 'What was it afterwards?' he asked. 'A joke?' And she addressed herself passionately to the arrogant profile.

'*No*—she was terrified that Howard would find out. He's terribly possessive. She's never had a holiday without him since they got married, and she married him when she was eighteen. He'd go spare if he knew. His mother ran away with another man when he was only a child and his father was very bitter about it. He never mentioned her name again, Howard's father, and Howard doesn't either. She died just before Howard and Celia were married and I never heard him call her anything but "That woman".'

'My God,' said Daniel quietly.

Lucy pleaded, 'Celia went on that holiday because she needed a break. She'd been working very hard. It was the election. She wasn't herself.' Heaven knows, she wasn't trying to be funny. 'I mean, it was so out of character, that fling with you and pretending to be me. You saw her tonight, didn't you?' That's the real Celia. She's a wonderful wife. She's a million miles from being a swinger.'

Daniel slowed down to consult a signpost and Lucy said, 'Next on the left.' The hedges were high and dark, and above them the sky was studded with stars like diamonds. If only Celia had filed down her nails and left off the diamonds perhaps he wouldn't have suspected, although he was asking.

'How long did you think you could get away with this?'

'We thought you'd only be here for two weeks.'

They reached the corner and as they rounded it he said, 'If I had been on holiday I'd have been back.'

'To see Celia?'

'To see you.'

She had to smile them. It meant that he wasn't angry. 'Were you fooled until tonight?' she asked.

'Certainly I was, at first, although there were some'— he grinned suddenly—'disparities. Some things that didn't add up. But we'd only spent a few hours together in Cyprus and it wasn't until I heard about your look-alike twin that I really began to wonder. Then there were the photographs that your mother showed me, and tonight clinched it.'

Lucy held out her hands, palms upraised, and when he nodded she said, 'I'm glad you know. It's been a strain. You won't say anything to anybody, will you?'

'Of course not.'

'Thank you.'

'For what?' She supposed that faithless wives and one-night stands were no great matter to him. He was a cynical sophisticated man, and she thought how sad it would have been if the girl called 'Lucy' who had let him make love to her in Cyprus had fallen in love with him. But as a companion he was great, and when he said, 'Will you come and see my house tomorrow?' she accepted promptly.

Of course he expected to be asked in when they reached her home and she had exaggerated the clerical work waiting for her. She could have spent the hour or two before bedtime with him, sitting comfortably together on the settee. Only bedtime would have followed, and she wasn't sure that she had the strength to keep him out of her bed. He was so disturbingly attractive, and she knew what his expert touch could do and shied from the memory. As the car drew up she said, 'I'm not going to ask you in.'

He looked exaggeratedly crestfallen. 'All that work waiting, is it? Maybe I could give you a hand.'

'I shouldn't think you'd be much help.'

She turned to open her door and he pulled her gently round and towards him so that she was warm and close in the circle of his arms. He looked down at her up-turned face, pushing aside the falling curtain of her hair, and began to kiss her, and she closed her mouth tightly and shook her head.

'Ah well,' he said. 'Tomorrow?'

Lucy was promising nothing for tomorrow, except that she would go along and see his house. But she nodded and he let her get out of the car, and she scuttled around it before he should decide to get out himself.

She had her door-key in the lock when she looked back, and he was still sitting in the car with the window down, the pale light of a street lamp glinting on him.

'Goodnight!' she called, and Daniel called back in his sexiest drawl, 'I could guarantee you a much better night if you'd ask me in.'

She hoped nobody was walking the dog or taking a late constitutional. She wouldn't want the neighbours to be hearing that, but she burst out laughing as she opened the door and let herself into the house.

There was nothing to worry about now. Celia's secret was safe, and Lucy should have slept peacefully. But she woke several times, and each time lay tossing and turning, asking herself what harm it could have done to let Daniel stay the night.

That was in the darkness, in the strange quiet hours when you don't think too clearly—only feel. And she felt very alone that night, which was unusual for Lucy ...

Daniel arrived next morning as she was washing up the cup and saucer and plate she had used for breakfast. She spotted him through the kitchen window, making for the back door, and she felt her spirits rise and a smile she couldn't suppress curved her lips.

'Do you usually come round the back of houses?' she asked, and he grinned,

'I thought I'd use the tradesman's entrance for a change.' That brought back the jokes she had shared with her father, and she wondered if her father would have liked Daniel. She thought that he would.

'It should be quite a nice day,' she said. The sun was rising in a cloudless sky, and Daniel assured her,

'It's going to be an absolutely splendid day.'

Lucy enjoyed most of it. They lunched well, at a

table set on the river bank, on fresh-caught trout with almonds, and most of the time it seemed to Lucy that they were laughing. He paid her crazy compliments, kissing her fingertips, brushing her face, her shoulders. Light caresses that felt like electricity on her skin.

She enjoyed having him near, and if she let him make love to her it might be the greatest thing she had ever known, a really sensational, mind-blowing experience. But it could also be a kind of madness, tearing her life apart. Not his life, just hers. Daniel would not be a good man to go overboard for, and Lucy was not risking peace of mind and pride in an affair that would almost certainly be as brief as it was passionate.

She flirted too, but always with a smile that said— don't believe a word of this, I'm no more in earnest than you are.

They understood each other well, and after lunch they set off for Lower Meon. They reached the village through winding lanes, the church spire pinpointing it across the fields and through the trees. It was typically Cotswold. The houses a mixture of thatched black-and-white and Cotswold stone, with a village green and ducks on a duckpond.

Daniel's house was stone. Roses and lavender bushes grew in the little front garden, and a splendid old purple wisteria framed the doorway. He had taken several pictures of Lucy during the day and now he said, 'Let's have one of you by the wisteria.' She stood still and smiled, and he clicked a couple of times, then slipped the camera back into his pocket and opened the door.

'Have you actually bought it,' she asked, as she stepped into the narrow flagstoned hall, 'or are you still considering?'

'I've paid up.'

She was pleased about that, because it was the kind of house she liked. There was a large low-ceilinged living room, with a stone fireplace, and a big kitchen in pine with pale yellow-topped surfaces. She could imagine copper pans in the kitchen, and the living room with its beams and inglenooks would be exciting to furnish. 'You can make this super,' she told him. 'What sort of furniture do you have?'

'Not much. How about keeping your eyes open at some auctions for me?'

'Yes, I'd love to.'

They went all over the house, from room to room, downstairs first, then up the little staircase into the three small bedrooms, discussing what might be put where. It was fun and it took ages. Daniel was prepared to spend quite a lot of money, and Lucy drew plans and made notes in a little notebook, and entered into the spirit of the thing so thoroughly that she might have been furnishing a home for herself.

When Daniel handed her a key she took it, then looked at it in the palm of her hand. 'Shall I need this?'

'I'll be away most of the time. If you get the furniture you could have it delivered here.'

'Supposing you don't like it?'

'I will.' If he didn't they could always sell it in the shop. She wouldn't buy anything that wasn't saleable. When they were back in the kitchen again she asked, 'Will you look after yourself?' If he was away a lot he'd have to be careful who he let into his home.

'Do you want the job?'

'I'm not a housekeeping lady.'

He laughed, 'I wasn't thinking about the house.'

And she laughed too. 'It's the house we're talking about.'

'In that case,' he said, 'I'll wait and see when I've got things sorted out.'

The electricity wasn't connected and they left at dusk, and Lucy turned down his suggestion of going back to his hotel with him. For dinner.

'I'd better get home,' she said, getting into the car,

and he held out his left wrist to show her his watch.

'It's only eight o'clock,' and she wrinkled her nose.

'But if I went back with you it would soon be nine, ten, eleven.'

'Why stop there?' His eyes gleamed with mischief and she nodded sagely,

'Exactly, that's why I'm not stopping anywhere. I'm going home.'

It was a game, nothing about it was serious. She wasn't being hooked by his charm. The competition would be too fierce. In the end there would be nothing but pain.

Maman was home because the lights were on, and Daniel said, 'I don't know that I'm up to your mother tonight.' Maman would have wanted to talk about Celia and Howard, and their beautiful home and their ideal marriage, and in the circumstances Lucy could understand how Daniel might have found that awkward.

'Lunch tomorrow?' he asked. 'I'll meet you in the Cheese Market at one o'clock,' and let her go without a goodnight kiss.

Maman greeted Lucy with a worried face and the information 'I should not be surprised if Celia was not sickening for the 'flu.'

Celia wasn't feeling well. She had brought Maman home after tea—the van was in the garage—Howard would be coming to collect her when she rang him, but she had had a headache all day, and now she was lying down on Lucy's bed. It seemed quite natural to Maman that Lucy should drop everything and rush upstairs to see how Celia was feeling now.

Celia was sitting up, looking pale in the fading light.

'How are you?' Lucy asked as she opened the door, and Celia hissed back,

'Did he stay here last night?'

She was still worrying about Daniel, that was the trouble, not incipient influenza. 'No.' Lucy closed the door and came to the bedside. 'He was here just after breakfast and we went out to lunch and then to look at the house.'

'What are you *doing*?' Celia's voice upped an octave. 'Going round to his house, going off in that caravan. *Why*?'

'I had a plan.' It had seemed a good idea at the time, and now Lucy sat down on the end of the bed and tried to make it sound reasonable again. 'He's too good-looking to be true, isn't he? and you told me he told you he could get any girl within twenty-four hours. He says he can't remember saying that, but it seems to me to sum him up fairly well. Well, I thought if I showed him that it wasn't on——' Celia started to speak, but Lucy continued,

'Yes, I know it was in Cyprus, but that was on holiday and folk often react differently on holiday. I thought if I played along but went on saying no to the serious stuff it would hit his ego and he wouldn't bother looking Lucy Friis up again.'

Celia demanded, 'Have you slept with him?' and when Lucy said no she said, 'You don't know much about men, do you?'

Lucy had never claimed to be an expert. She supposed she was about average for most girls her age, but Celia sounded scornful. 'You know what you've done? You've thrown out a challenge. Oh, he'll have to add you to his score now. He won't rest till he does.'

That was a chilling thought. Lucy could feel the warmth ebbing from her as though her blood was turning to ice. 'And if I couldn't say no,' Celia went on, 'what makes you think that you'll hold out for long? I had so many more reasons not to play around.'

Lucy knew them all, but Celia didn't know that the masquerade was over. She had to be told; Lucy said quietly, 'He's guessed it wasn't me in Cyprus. It was our hands mainly. Were you wearing your wedding ring out there?'

'Of course.' Celia gave a convulsive little sob and Lucy tried a weak joke.

'He won't say anything. He doesn't want Howard coming after him with a gun.'

'Howard wouldn't do that!' as though Lucy had been serious. 'That would finish his career. Howard wouldn't have a scandal for anything, but I don't suppose he'd ever forgive me. I hate Daniel Stewart! I can't stand the sight or the sound of him. Lucy, finish with him.' She reached for Lucy's hand and held it tight. 'He's just a womaniser. Please Lucy, *please*...!'

Daniel was talking to a girl, when Lucy walked towards the stone arches of Moreton Meadows Medieval Cheese Market on Monday lunchtime. The girl wore jeans and a green shirt. She had short crisp dark hair and she was standing with one hand on her hip in a consciously provocative stance, smiling up at him.

Lucy quickened her step instinctively, but then she slowed down because she wasn't competing, any girl could have him so far as she was concerned, although she still sounded strained when she reached them and said, 'Hello there.'

'Hello,' said Daniel, and turned his smile on her, and she wished that she didn't have to do this. She wished she could have let things take their natural course.

'Down this road and opposite the Crown,' said the girl. 'Thanks,' and she walked away with swinging hips and a lingering backwards smile until she bumped into another pedestrian.

'What did she want?' Lucy murmured—as if I didn't know.

'The Cobweb Tearooms,' said Daniel. Women would be asking him directions for years to come. Any girl who loved him would need a sense of humour, and right now Lucy couldn't believe that she was ever going to feel like laughing again.

'Shall we eat at the Crown,' he was asking her. 'Or is there anywhere else you prefer? That we can get into.'

It was midday and the town was full and Lucy said,

'I can't manage lunch.'

'Dinner?'

'No.' She had to explain that she couldn't manage anything, now or ever, but with the holidaymakers shoving around them all she could do was bite her lip, and Daniel took her elbow, guiding her, and she dragged back until he pointed out, 'We can't talk here.'

She didn't ask where they were going, and they walked as fast as the crowds allowed, along the main road and down a side street to where he had parked his car. He opened the door and told a coasting motorist, looking for a parking spot, 'Sorry, we're not moving out.'

Lucy's mouth felt full of ashes and it was stifling hot in here. She didn't look at Daniel. She stared ahead at the car almost bumper to bumper in front, but she didn't see that either.

'I can understand why you were anxious to get rid of me when you were doing your double act,' he said when he was seated beside her, 'but why now?'

'Because'—she twisted her fingers together—'Celia is going to make herself ill if she goes on like this. Her conscience is playing hell with her and every time she sees you she's going to hate herself.'

'I'm sorry about that, but——'

'Please, just keep away from us.' Her voice was low and quite controlled. 'I really don't want any more of you.' She wasn't being added to his score. 'You're quite a guy and you know it, and it's amusing for a while, but I think the game's played out.'

'What game?' Daniel sounded baffled. The conceit of him, thinking he'd fooled her that any of it was serious. Sex was a game to him. She doubted if the word 'love' was in his vocabulary.

'You know it's a game,' she snapped, 'and to be honest——'

'Yes, let's be honest.' The sun was bright on the

windscreen and his eyes were slits under heavy lids. He was leaning back in his seat, turned towards her, one hand on the wheel, with that easy relaxed animal grace.

'To be honest,' Lucy said crisply, 'if I hadn't been covering for Celia I wouldn't have gone anywhere or done anything with you, because you are not my kind of man.'

'No?' His lips hardly moved, then he began to smile, and she felt herself blushing at the memory of those moments when her treacherous senses had responded to his kiss as hungrily as though she had been starved. It was a warning of the power he might have over her unless she broke away, quickly and finally, and she babbled,

'As you've gathered, I'm not Celia, and I'm not really like Celia. You set out to get her and——'

'Who says?' That threw her because it was so obvious.

'Well, of course you did!' she shrilled. 'She told me how it happened. And, come to that, she was wearing a wedding ring.'

'Come to that, she was not.'

'That's a stupid lie!' Celia would never take off her wedding ring. Perhaps he had forgotten. But his expression was cynical and the line of his mouth was hard as he said softly,

'You're the stupid one, sweetheart. I'm no monk, but your sister's no saint. She might be a wife in a million here, but she was on offer in Cyprus.'

Lucy felt as though he had hit her between the eyes, jerking her head back in a flash of roaring pain. Her hand lifted convulsively and her anger was so fierce that it seemed as though she had struck out, and she half expected to see a red weal rise on his cheek.

She turned away, sickened, her hand dropping. 'That's a foul thing to say! You disgust me—you're despicable!'

'Don't be so mealy-mouthed.' He sounded bored now, and her anger turned cold.

She looked at him with all the contempt she could muster. 'Oh, I could make it a lot stronger than that. Lord, I hate your sort! You're so bigheaded, so self-centred.' The haughty handsome face didn't flinch, and she sneered, 'If you didn't have that face what would you be?'

He shrugged, 'A skeleton?'

He was laughing at her. He probably thought she was an even bigger joke than Celia, and she couldn't get the car door open fast enough. 'Goodbye,' he said, as she slammed the door making the passers-by jump.

Lucy strode away, hurrying through the chattering crowds as though he might be following. He wasn't, of course. She walked alone, racked by conflicting emotions. She had done the right thing, taken the only way out, and yet she had this horrible reaction of deep, deep loss that seemed to be draining the life out of her.

CHAPTER EIGHT

In the short time since Lucy had met him Daniel had practically filled her life, but she was unprepared for the vacuum he would leave. It was almost as though somebody who had been with her for ever had gone.

Celia was glad. When Lucy rang from the office on Monday afternoon and told her she said, 'Thank God for that! Now perhaps we'll have some peace. All I want to do is forget he ever happened.'

It wasn't going to be easy for Lucy. She found herself thinking about Daniel continually. Puzzling, because it was true that he wasn't her kind, and yet every time the phone rang, and it wasn't Daniel, she felt oddly let down.

Maman asked about him, of course. 'Are you seeing Daniel tonight?' she wanted to know on Monday evening when Lucy came home from work, and Lucy said,

'Not tonight nor any night, and it's my decision and it's final.'

Maman did one of her deep resigned sighs, and Lucy knew what she was thinking before she said, 'You never make the best of yourself like Celia does. Celia would have——' She would have gone on to say, 'Celia could have held him. Celia could have made him marry her.' Something like that, if Lucy hadn't interrupted,

'I don't want to talk about it. It's over. It's finished. He's gone.'

Maman sighed again. 'So I don't suppose he will be taking my picture. Howard said it would have been quite an honour.'

'There are plenty of good portrait photographers around,' Lucy pointed out. 'I'm sure that Howard could recommend somebody else.'

On market day Ma Morris shouted across as soon as she saw Lucy, 'Your young man not back, then?' He had been in London last week, this morning, for all Lucy knew, he might stroll along and turn up at her pitch, so she smiled brightly and called back,

'Not so far as I know, and he isn't my young man.' But the day went by with no sign of Daniel, and although trade was quite good nothing was the fun it had been the day he had helped out on the stall.

Neither Aunt Dolly nor Uncle Joe asked any questions. Not even when Lucy went to the cinema with someone else on Wednesday evening. And that wasn't a success, because although she tried to concentrate on the nice-enough young man who had paid for her cinema seat, and the Chinese meal they ate afterwards, she kept seeing Daniel. She blinked so often, clearing her vision and her mind, that Trevor enquired if she had something in her eye.

'In my head,' she could have said. Not in her heart, of course. It was just that she couldn't get Daniel out of her mind. He was unscrupulous—saying that about Celia—selfish, superficial; but for the first time in her life she had a crush that was making her absolutely miserable, and all she could do was wait for it to end. It would, of course. There was no question of her being really in love with the man.

On Monday morning, before the shop opened, she was sitting at the desk in the office, opening the mail, and out of one typewritten envelope, post-dated London, addressed to her, she took a letter signed 'Daniel.'

Her heart gave a great leap and started thudding in her rib cage, and her gasp was loud enough to bring Aunt Dolly round the desk, asking, 'Who's it from? What is it?'

'Daniel,' said Lucy faintly, and although Aunt Dolly had been a model of discretion up to now she couldn't resist pouncing on a second smaller folded piece of paper that had dropped from the envelope, and that turned out to be a sizeable cheque made out to Lucy.

'He'll be away for a few weeks,' Lucy read, 'and in the meantime will I start furnishing the house.'

Aunt Dolly knew about the house, but she didn't know about the list in Lucy's notebook. Nobody did. And now Lucy had to explain and Aunt Dolly wanted to know why she hadn't told them before, and Lucy said it was because since then they'd said goodbye and this was not personal. But as a business arrangement she supposed it could stand.

'If he's letting you choose his furniture,' said Aunt Dolly with a knowing nod, 'he must have a lot of faith in your taste.'

'Only for furniture,' said Lucy. 'He knows I go to the auctions and I know the dealers. We've done this kind of thing for customers before.'

'Have we?' asked Aunt Dolly, although they were often asked to look out for items. 'Will you store it here?'

'I've—I've got a key to the house.' She would have handed it back if she hadn't stormed off on Monday. She had intended to post it, of course, but she still had it at the bottom of her handbag.

Her first reaction, when she saw his signature, had been delight, but she sobered down very quickly. Taking this assignment was no way to break free of Daniel, and Celia was probably right. His pride was keeping him after her until he had her, and then she wouldn't be the girl who got away any more, and he wouldn't particularly care whether she stayed or went.

But he was away for several weeks. That would give her the chance to do some furniture shopping. She'd like to, it was a fascinating old house. And by the time Daniel came back her infatuation should have worn itself out.

She took the letter to Uncle Joe, with her notes and the cheque, and he looked at them all several times. Then he said, 'It's up to you.'

She was perched on the end of his workbench and she began to explain very earnestly, 'I wouldn't buy anything that we couldn't get rid of if he didn't want it. So it couldn't do any harm, could it? We're buying all the time, aren't we? I'd just keep the list by me and if anything turned up——'

'Like I said,' said Uncle Joe, 'it's up to you.'

Lucy decided to go ahead. Well, it *couldn't* do any harm, and it might be fun. There was a table and chair right here in the storeroom that she might try out for a start, and she loaded them into her van and when she finished work for the day she went over to Daniel's house.

No one was around, it was very quiet, and as she turned the key in the front door she thought it might be a good idea to buy a home for herself, if she didn't marry in the next few years. She had a nice home with Maman, and another with Uncle Joe and Aunt Dolly, but she would love a house like this. She went into the living room, remembering what kind of furniture she had been asked to keep a look-out for, seeing it so plainly in her mind that, when she stood at the window with her back to the room, it felt as though the house was already lived in. She could imagine the softness of a rug beneath her feet, and the scent of roses seemed in the room, not just outside in the garden.

She was standing as though she was waiting, but of course there was nobody coming; she wondered where Daniel was, and decided he was probably taking pictures of fashion models in some exotic faraway place. That stabbed as fiercely as jealousy, and she shook herself out of her reverie and went back to the van to fetch the table and chair.

She placed them both in the window, a large wooden armchair and a small round polished table, and they looked fine, she thought. Tomorrow she would bring an oil lamp to put on the table. There wasn't one on her list, but all the same she would bring the lamp out of the caravan.

Most evenings she slipped over to the house, because most evenings she had something to add. When the items were cumbersome Uncle Joe came and helped her to unload and put them into place. The four-poster bed was her pride and joy; when she returned from an auction with that she was delighted with herself.

Uncle Joe liked the house, although he looked thoughtful when he saw Lucy wandering around as though she owned it. There was no reason for him to worry. She knew it could never be her house, but it was pleasant to have the key, to find things that would suit it, and sometimes to light the lamp and sit there a while in the shadows.

Neighbours noticed her and she explained what she was doing, but couldn't satisfy their curiosity because she simply didn't know when Daniel planned to take up residence. She was going to be sorry when he did come back and she had to hand over the key, because in a strange secret way the house was becoming very important to her. She hadn't mentioned what she was doing to Maman, nor to Celia, but sometimes when she opened the door and stepped into the little hall she could feel a welcome wrapping around her like strong loving arms.

She was happy, even in the empty rooms. She would walk around them, imagining how they were going to look, and sometimes at night before she left she would stand at the front door, framed by the deep purple wisteria, reluctant to leave. As though she should be staying, she should be waiting a little longer.

She did a lot of work, she was kept busy, but her social life, that had always been a lively affair, had quietened down because she couldn't work up any enthusiasm for the men who had been her dates. She pretended she was having a riotous time, booked up every night, but her excuses were fiction. She just didn't want to be bothered with them, although before long she would simply have to make an effort and start getting out and about again.

As the days went by she was almost sure that her infatuation for Daniel was waning. Nobody ever mentioned him. Celia seemed to have put the whole matter out of her mind. When Lucy saw her the talk was like it used to be, nothing about Daniel or Cyprus. Maman never brought his name up again either, and Lucy was telling herself she was almost free of the physical pull that had nearly ensnared her.

Then, on a Friday, just over a month after she last saw him, he phoned the shop. She was in the workshed, working out a new design on a large white sheet of cartridge paper, when Aunt Dolly came in and said, 'Daniel just rang, but he said not to bother you.'

Not to bother her! That was a laugh, because her heart jumped like it had when she'd seen his name at the end of that letter. Worse than then. 'I told him you'd been getting things for his house,' said Aunt Dolly, 'and he seemed very pleased. He'll be along on Monday.'

'Where is he now?' Lucy croaked, and Aunt Dolly said,

'I didn't have time to ask. I'd better get back, there are folk in the shop.'

Lucy kept her head bowed over her work and Uncle Joe said nothing at all, and she didn't know whether she was thrilled to bits or scared stiff, but for the rest of the afternoon she didn't make much progress with the new design.

She told Maman over tea. Celia and the children had been over on Friday afternoon as usual, leaving before Lucy got home, and tea was the sandwiches and sponge cake and pâté and salad they hadn't eaten. Friday was always left-over tea for Lucy, and as she nibbled on a lettuce leaf she said, 'Daniel rang to say he'll be calling in the shop on Monday.'

'Will he?' Maman didn't sound very interested. Celia had brought some new snapshots of the family and Maman had them spread out on a small table. She was picking them up and putting them down as though she was playing patience with them.

'Maybe he'll take your photograph now,' said Lucy, and Maman almost shuddered.

'No, thank you, dear, I don't like his kind of photographs.'

Lucy's jaw dropped. 'What *do* you mean?'

'They are not nice pictures,' said her mother. 'Howard showed me one in a newspaper the other day and it made me feel quite dreadful.'

Lucy gulped and choked. 'Whatever was it?'

'Refugees. A child.' Maman looked at the smiling face of her own small granddaughter. 'Somewhere where there is a war. It was so sad, it almost made me cry.'

'Those are the kind of pictures Daniel takes?'

'That was the one Howard showed me.' Maman never lingered over unpleasant things for long. She went on briskly, 'And Celia says it is much better that you are not interested in him because he does not have a very good reputation. Too many lady friends. Celia says you should forget all about him.'

'Very likely,' said Lucy.

She went to the phone and dialled Celia's number, got the housekeeper and asked for Howard. 'What sort of photographs does Daniel Stewart take?' she asked him.

'Don't you know?'

Howard's surprise was understandable. She was surprised herself that she had taken it for granted that Daniel's work would be pretty and glossy and shallow. She said, 'When I told you he did mostly fashion work you just smiled.'

'I thought you were joking. Perhaps he does, sometimes, but that certainly isn't his forte. You don't know?' Howard was still astounded. 'You've been going around with him and you really don't know what he does?'

But she hadn't been 'going around'. Well, only for a little while, although it was beginning to feel that those few days had been most of her life. And how many photographers' names did she know? Lord Snowdon, Patrick Lichfield, David What's-his-name. It wasn't like someone on TV or a bylined journalist. Photographers, even good ones, were mostly anonymous men.

She asked, 'Is he good?'

'There are few better,' said Howard. 'Haven't you seen *any* of his pictures?'

'No, I haven't. He didn't talk about his work, and I only met him just before he came round to your house and he's been away somewhere for the last month. Maman says you showed her something in the paper last week.'

Howard remembered it, but, 'That won't still be in the house. You wouldn't have the colour supplements, would you, about a couple of months back? No, of course you wouldn't, but I think I have. I believe I kept that one, there was an article on education in it. If you want to see it——'

'I do,' said Lucy. 'I'll come now ...'

She could taste the dust and the heat and the despair as she turned the pages. The subject was an earthquake in Peru, and you were there. Towering ruins threatened to crash down on you so that you cowered. A child's smashed toy tore at your heart. And the people. Each face, each posture, told their story, but always with such understanding and compassion that they seemed to be speaking, telling it.

Daniel cared when he was here, she thought, he cared like hell; and she could see him, dirty and dishevelled and weary, with no thought for himself or his safety. This was the man behind the mask and she should have been stunned. But she wasn't. It was right. She looked up at Howard, who had stood watching her.

'Marvellous, aren't they?' said Howard. 'They must have made a lot of difference to the relief appeal.'

After a few moments she managed to get the words past the lump in her throat. 'What was the picture you showed Maman? Where was it? She said somewhere where a war was.'

He said the name of an emergent state, torn by bloody revolution, and Lucy bit back a cry. She had watched it happening on television, read newspaper reports and seen photographs, and all the time Daniel had been there. Her face turned pale with fear for him, then she whispered, 'He's back now, though.' Pleading with Howard, 'He wouldn't have phoned from there, would he? He'd be in London or somewhere like that before he phoned, wouldn't he?'

'Oh, I should think so,' Howard said reassuringly, and teased her, 'I thought you said he was nothing special to you.'

'But he is special, isn't he?' said Lucy, and Howard smiled.

'Good luck, then, but I ought to warn you he's considered a confirmed bachelor.'

'I remember him telling me something of the sort.' She almost managed a smile, and thought—I love him. He isn't for marriage, he probably isn't for love, but I love him, so please God keep him safe.

She went on looking at the photographs until Celia came into the room. Celia knew why Lucy was here, but when Howard had produced the colour supplement Celia had said she had a couple of phone calls to make. After about ten minutes she came back, drawing Howard's attention to the little carriage clock on the mantelpiece. He was making a speech somewhere to-night, and he said, 'It's all right, dear, I'm in plenty of time.' But he kissed her goodbye, and brushed Lucy's cheek in brotherly fashion, and went off to his meeting.

Lucy had laid the magazine down beside her on the sofa and Celia picked it up, as the door closed after Howard, demanding, 'What on earth did you want to look at these for?'

'I wanted to see what kind of photographs he took,' said Lucy.

'Why should that matter?' Celia gave the pages a brief glance and shut the magazine, with a shrug of distaste just like Maman's.

'They show the kind of person he is,' said Lucy, and Celia looked blank, then said sharply,

'I've told you the kind of person he is.'

But Celia didn't know, and never would. 'He's coming back on Monday,' said Lucy.

'You're pleased about that?'

'Yes, I am.'

'Of course, if he hadn't come back you could have gone after him, couldn't you?' Lucy stared, less at the sentiment than at Celia's hot cheeks and the angry brightness of her eyes as she snapped, 'You've always been able to please yourself what you do,' and she sounded bitterly resentful. 'I'm the one who's always been trapped.'

'*Trapped?*' Lucy echoed, and Celia scowled like a sulky child.

'You can go anywhere, do anything. I've got Maman and Howard always breathing down my neck. I've always envied you, I suppose that's why I gave him your name, because I wanted to be you for a bit, you can do anything you want to do.' Discontent puckered her mouth. 'But I was good at art too, you know. I'd probably have made a better painter than you have, if they hadn't got me married off.'

Lucy sat very still, then she said very quietly, 'Nobody made you stop painting. Why don't you——?'

'It's too late now,' said Celia, and when Lucy pointed out, 'You're twenty-two, not seventy-two,' 'Oh, you don't understand! Nobody bothers to understand me.'

She picked up the magazine. 'Well, I've warned you about Daniel, I can't do any more, and you'll please yourself anyway, you always do. I don't want to talk about it. I think you'd better go home now.' She thrust the colour supplement into Lucy's hands with a glare of pure venom. 'And please take these horrid pictures with you!'

Lucy drove away from the house quickly, and drew up in the first pull-off about half a mile down the road. She was shaking. Celia was her twin, her much-loved sister, but she had looked at her just now as though she hated her. The magazine on the passenger seat had fallen open at the centre spread of Daniel's pictures. One was the face of a young boy who had lost his family, and Lucy felt the same pain that was in his eyes.

Celia had practically thrown her out of the house. What if she couldn't go back again, couldn't see the children? Would Celia do that to her? Could she?

What was she going to do now? She couldn't go home, because Maman would never understand how she could have quarrelled with Celia, and she couldn't tell Maman what Celia had said. But she could tell Aunt Dolly. As a child Lucy had always got her hugs and her comforting there, and she looked up and down the empty road, making sure that it was safe to pull out.

She drove very carefully indeed, to counteract the jitters, and when her van was safely parked behind the shop she sat for a moment, head back and eyes closed, as though she had come to shore after a hard swim. Then she picked up magazine and handbag and let herself in through the side door.

Uncle Joe and Aunt Dolly were in the living room. He had a newspaper and she had a book, and Lucy smiled brightly and said, 'Hello, can you be doing with me for the evening? There's a bit of family fuss on.'

She saw the look they exchanged and then Uncle Joe

got up and said, 'I'll just see to—er—yes, I'll do that,' and went out, and Aunt Dolly waited until the door was closed and Lucy was sitting down before she asked quietly,

'Is it Daniel?'

'No, not really.' Partly perhaps. Cyprus seemed to have started it, although Celia must have felt this way about Lucy before then. Lucy let her shoulderbag slip to the floor, and held the rolled-up magazine tightly in her hands. She said, in a quick husky voice, 'It's Celia. She ought to be happy, oughtn't she, but she says I'm the lucky one. Because I work for my living she seems to think I have a wonderful life. She told me to get out of her house tonight. I think—she hates me.'

Aunt Dolly looked neither shocked nor surprised. 'No, she doesn't,' she said. 'She envies you. She'd like what you've got and what she's got. She's like your mother. They don't know what real contentment is.'

There was no malice in Aunt Dolly, but there was a great depth of understanding, and when Lucy whispered, 'They don't really love me, do they?' she said,

'Oh, but they do, and they always will. In their way.'

It was Aunt Dolly who had been a mother to her, Uncle Joe, her father's friend, who had watched over her like a father, and Lucy smiled with trembling lips and said, 'Yes, well, thank God I've got you.'

'And Daniel's coming back on Monday.'

That steadied Lucy's smile, although she had to admit that she didn't have Daniel. 'I'll tell you something,' said Aunt Dolly. 'Joe didn't realise he loved me until I told him.'

Lucy had to laugh a little at that. She believed it too, she could see it happening, but she couldn't see anyone having to tell Daniel how he felt about anything, and she said ruefully, 'Daniel's his own man. I don't suppose he's thought about me much these last few weeks, much less missed me. Look at these!' and she opened the magazine. 'And do you know where he's been this last month?'

Later she phoned Maman to say where she was, and that she was stopping the night. She usually stayed on Fridays to be ready for market early on Saturday. 'I may stay over the weekend,' she said. 'I've a lot of work here.'

'All right dear,' said Maman. 'I will expect you when I see you.'

Lucy's work was getting Daniel's house ready for him, and she needed all the free time she had between now and Monday. Or even Sunday. He'd said he'd call in the shop on Monday, but he could be arriving earlier than that, and surely the first thing he would do would be to go round and see how Lucy had spent his money. Aunt Dolly had told him she had been buying furniture. He must be anxious to know what the house was looking like, and she wanted to be there when he came.

She concentrated on the big living room. She had enough to make that look almost fully furnished. Small pieces—assorted chairs, a padded footstool, a jewel-red Turkish rug to lay on the flagstones before the inglenook fireplace. Then there was a leather-topped desk, a couple of large leather armchairs, an oak chest, and a small chesterfield that would need re-covering but was sound and quite comfortable. And the table with the lamp in the window.

All she left upstairs was her best buy, the four-poster in carved oak, and when she went along after market on Saturday she took bedding and made up the bed. Daniel could stay here now. He'd need to get the electricity turned on, but he could sleep here in comfort and he could get his meals at the village pub.

She returned to Aunt Dolly's late on Saturday evening. After eleven o'clock at night Daniel wasn't turning up, so there was no sense in hanging around. She told herself that she hadn't expected him yet, but she was still disappointed. She had a meal ready, including one of Aunt Dolly's pork pies, and the Primus stove from the caravan to make coffee, and a bottle of wine, and she sat at the window in the wooden armchair until it was nearly midnight.

Then she looked at the chesterfield and wondered if she should curl up on that and spend the night here, because he might arrive quite early in the morning. No one would worry, Maman wasn't expecting her and Aunt Dolly would decide she had gone home. But it would be a cramped night's rest, and she would be a wreck tomorrow, and she could come back early.

She threw a cloth over the little round table, laid with the food, and left it and climbed wearily into her van. She was sure that Daniel would be glad to be welcomed. She had a fire laid with logs in the inglenook too, she could have that alight in a matter of minutes. It would all look lovely. He would be pleased to see the house alive and waiting for him, but she didn't want him thinking that she had taken it on herself to move in.

He might not mind. There was room. He might be happy to have her around, or he might think it was a heck of a cheek. He might have other ideas—someone else sharing; another girl. She put the key into her bag and wondered how she would feel when she had to hand it back.

When I get my own little house, she promised herself, then I'll have my own key, and I can start looking for furniture for myself. I'll paint some of it, of course, and maybe I'll have the screen that Daniel liked when he saw it in the shop that first night. It was still there, it hadn't been sold, the winding lane going over the hill like the lanes they had travelled in the vardo.

But next morning she loaded the screen into the van. At breakfast she had said to Aunt Dolly and Uncle Joe, 'I thought I'd like to give Daniel something I'd painted as a housewarming present. I thought perhaps the screen.' And they'd agreed it was a nice thought, so she was taking it for Daniel's home instead of keeping it for the little house she might some day be buying for herself.

She stood it in the corner of the living room. At least with that there he could never quite forget her, and to-day she was sure that he would be coming home.

It was a damp day. She wished the sun would shine to make everything look bright and cheerful, instead of this grey sky and fine drizzle of rain. She was tempted to light the fire, but she had only brought a few logs and she didn't want to waste them. She wanted a few hours of merry crackling warmth when Daniel came.

She picked roses in the morning, a great fragrant arm-ful wet with dew, and stood them on the desk in a big terracotta jug she had brought from Aunt Dolly's. She warmed up a tin of soup for herself at midday, and she set the table for two again.

Late afternoon she went to a phone kiosk in the mid-dle of the village and rang Maman. Daniel might have phoned there. He had told Aunt Dolly not to bother Lucy when he called the shop on Thursday, but he might have tried to get in touch Friday or yesterday. Maman said there had been a call this morning, and Lucy's heart had time to skip a beat before she went on, 'Trevor.'

'Oh!' said Lucy.

'And Celia,' said Maman.

'Oh,' said Lucy again.

'I hope you haven't been upsetting Celia,' said Maman severely. 'She asked me to tell you that she's sorry if she sounded cross on Thursday night. She says she hopes you didn't take offence at anything she said, because she didn't mean it. Now what was that all about?'

'She didn't like Daniel's photographs,' said Lucy, and Maman gave a muted shriek.

'Neither did I—such ugly pictures! What a silly thing to be upsetting yourselves over!'

'If you see her before I do,' said Lucy, 'tell her I've forgotten whatever it was we did say.'

'I should hope so,' said Maman.

Lucy was sure that Celia would forget. Like Maman, Celia could shut unpleasant things out of her mind. She would blot out the memories of Cyprus as she had done before, but she had been scared when Daniel turned up and it was unlikely she would run wild again.

She needed the cushioned luxury of her life. In her way Celia loved Howard, and she loved Lucy, but it was a selfish loving. They couldn't help it, Celia and Maman, it was their nature, and Lucy felt she must always have known that her mother and sister had no real depth of feeling.

Unlike her father. Unlike her, although she was only now discovering how deeply and completely she could fall in love. This was the first time, and the last. For better, for worse, and for ever, it was Daniel; and as the long day dragged on she paced the house longing for him with a real physical ache, that had her on the edge of tears when night fell and there was still no sign of him.

She wouldn't accept he wasn't coming. She had been so sure he would, although perhaps it didn't make all that much sense. He might not be coming down this way at all until tomorrow. Or if he did come today he might go straight to an hotel and leave looking at the furniture until Monday. He didn't know anybody would be waiting for him here, he'd think it was a dark and empty house, so why should he come dashing round?

Perhaps she had a streak of Maman and Celia in her, she reflected wryly, she wouldn't face facts either. But the disappointment today was so bitter that she couldn't bear to face it. She couldn't be here tomorrow. She had to go back to the shop because Daniel had said he would call in there, and then she could come round to the house with him, of course, but it wouldn't be the way she'd planned it. She'd wanted so desperately to be waiting, for him to come home and find her here.

It was dark now. He wouldn't come to a house with no electricity after dark. Nobody had told him there was a lamp burning and a fire that only needed a match. She opened the front door and looked out of a silent world, and felt the loneliness she had known, when she stood in the ring of the Dancers, closing in on her. This was how it would be, life without Daniel, all this emptiness.

Her eyes were full of tears. She felt them sliding down her cheeks and shook her head to shake them away. What good did she think it was going to do, standing here sniffling on the doorstep? 'Damn you,' she hiccuped. 'Why don't you come? Oh, Daniel, *please*, please come *home*!'

But he wasn't coming and she might as well go. She'd make some coffee first, and when the kettle boiled she filled her flask and took it into the living room, then sat on the chesterfield and told herself she'd wait ten more minutes and then she'd go.

She wanted to cry her eyes out, but if she did that with her luck today Aunt Dolly would be waiting up when she got back, and red eyes wouldn't get past her. She curled into the corner, her head on her arm, and when she began to feel sleepy she let herself drift off. Sleep killed time and she had nothing else to do with the hours ahead, but when she woke she had a crick in the neck and her back took some straightening.

She did not feel like driving back; and if she didn't watch it she was going to start crying. She had never been a girl for tears, she didn't know they were so hard to hold back. She was going to bed, she'd leave early in the morning when it was light. Right now she was going to bed to sleep, and she was *not* going to cry.

The lamp was still burning in the window. She had

filled it before she lit it, when dusk started to fall. 'Carry on,' she said, 'I can use the company.' She left it where it was, on the little table, then went upstairs in the darkness, into the room of the four-poster, kicked off her shoes and took off sweater and skirt and got between the sheets.

'Go to sleep,' she told herself. 'Go—to—sleep,' and she lay watching the window and wondering how long it would be before she saw the first grey streaks of dawn. Sometimes she heard a car. Even through villages, even at night, there were still cars, or lorries or whatever they were.

Once she thought one of them was slowing down. Of course it wasn't, but she raised herself on an elbow, straining to hear, then lights flashed across her window, and she was out of bed at the speed of light, flinging back the bedclothes, almost falling down the stairs.

She had the front door open as Daniel reached it, gabbling, 'Hello, I haven't moved in, I just hung around until it was too late to go. Come in, come in!'

She had the door of the living room open and she rushed to put a match to the fire, then realised what time it was—who wanted a fire lit at this hour?—and dropped the matches. 'I've got coffee,' she said. 'It's here somewhere,' and she went down on her knees by the chesterfield.

Daniel was standing in the doorway looking across at her. She held up the coffee flask, and he came over and sat down and she looked up at him in the lamplight. There were dark shadows round the eyes and under the high cheekbones. He looked gaunt and exhausted, and she whispered, 'You look terrible.'

Then the familiar smile flashed. 'Thank you, lady.'

'Are you all right?' She wasn't smiling.

'Tired,' he said, 'that's all.' He reached to touch her face, very gently. 'Now you look beautiful,' he said.

'Was it bad?' Of course it was bad. Hell is bad. That was a silly question, but he answered her.

'It nearly always is, we live in bad times, but when I look at you I feel there's hope for the world.' He held out his arms and she went into them, and he hugged the breath out of her, and her arms were around his neck as tightly as though he was keeping her afloat in a shoreless sea.

Lucy didn't know how long they clung together. She could hear her own heart throbbing, and his, and she just held on to him because she had never in all her life been so rapturously happy. At last he said, 'This is the first peace I've known since you got out of my car.'

'Why didn't you follow me?' She rubbed her cheek against his. 'Why did you let me go?'

'I didn't see what I could do. You were angry about Celia, you thought I was a conceited slob.' Her lips twitched. 'What *could* I do? I had to leave next day. I thought—give her time to calm down, and she might even miss me, a little.'

'Yes,' she said, and turned her face to put her lips to his cheek.

'I've missed you.' He held her a little away, looking at her as though he could look for ever. 'It's never happened before, I never missed anyone like that. I've thought about you. I've carried you with me.'

'Have you?' she whispered.

'Literally.' He fished into an inner pocket for a wallet, and took out the photographs he had taken the last time they were here, of her standing at the front door. 'I've looked at these a hundred times,' he told her, 'and told myself you were doing that, standing there, waiting for me.'

She had been, night after night. 'I was going to drive down tomorrow,' he said. 'I was booked into a hotel, but just before we landed I looked at these and I felt that you were saying, "Come home." So I did.' He would have grinned if she had laughed. He was not sure if he was making a fool of himself, but that was exactly what had happened, and she said,

'If you hadn't come I'd have cried all night.'

'It *is* home, isn't it?' His hands tightened on her, and it was the house she loved more than any other, but anywhere Daniel was would be her home: a vardo, a hotel, a foreign land. She asked shakily,

'How do you feel about camp-followers?'

He took a deep breath. 'Marry me, it sounds better.'

She wanted to shout *'Yes!'* and go on shouting until it echoed all over the silent countryside, but she had to say, 'I thought marriage wasn't for you.'

'So did I,' he said simply. 'The state the world's in it seemed safer not to care too much for anybody. My parents died together in a plane, but if one had gone first the other would have followed. They couldn't have existed apart. I've never seen it with anyone else, but that's how I feel about you, it's the way I want you, for ever.'

He looked at her then as though he pleaded for his life. 'Lucy my love, please will you try to love me?'

It would take a lifetime to show how much she loved him. For now she could only whisper, 'I do,' and it sounded like part of the marriage service, and he lifted her hand and kissed it and promised,

'I'll make you happy, and I'll keep you safe as long as there's breath in me.'

'As long as you love me I'm safe.' She laughed softly. 'I could even stand in the middle of the Dancers and not be scared.'

'Last time,' he said, 'I'd have given all I had to have put my arms around you and told you not to be afraid.'

The last time, when he had put his arms around her, she had fought like a wild thing, but tonight there would be no battle. She was on fire for him, his mouth was burning on her skin, and she gave a little strangled sob of joy as the hard lean body came down on her. 'I love you,' she gasped. 'Oh, I love you so.'

'I love you,' he said huskily, and then, 'Good grief!'

'W-what?'

'The room's furnished!' He looked around the lamp-lit room, and Lucy stared up at him.

'Of course it is. You knew I'd been finding furniture. I brought you the screen, and what did you think this was?' She poked the back of the chesterfield with her elbow, and he grinned,

'I didn't see it. I didn't see anything but you.'

'Quite right,' she said. 'Wait a minute.' His lips were a fraction from hers and there was a lump in the chesterfield in the small of her back. 'My best buy's upstairs,' she said. 'In the master bedroom. I want to show it to you.'

'Now?'

'There'll never be a better time.' She wriggled free, smiling, her eyes shining. 'I'll show you,' she said. 'Come and I'll show you,' and she took his hand and led him up the stairs into the moonlit dark.

NEW!

HARLEQUIN SUPERROMANCE

LOVE'S EMERALD FLAME

WILLA LAMBERT

A Contemporary Love Story

The steaming jungle of Peru was the stage
for their love. Diana Green, a spirited
and beautiful young journalist, who became
a willing pawn in a dangerous game...
and Sloane Hendriks, a lonely desperate
man, driven by a secret he would
reveal to no one.

Love's Emerald Flame is the second stunning novel in
this timely new series of modern love stories—
HARLEQUIN SUPERROMANCES.

Longer, exciting, sensual and dramatic, these
compelling new books are for you—the woman of today!

HARLEQUIN SUPERROMANCE #2, Love's Emerald Flame,
wherever paperback books are sold
or order your copy from

Harlequin Reader Service

In U.S.A.
MPO Box 707
Niagara Falls, NY 14302

In Canada
649 Ontario St.
Stratford, Ont. N5A 6W2

SPECIAL

Harlequin Romance Treasury Book Offer

This superb Romance Treasury is yours at little or <u>no</u> cost.

3 exciting, full-length Romance novels in one beautiful hard-cover book.

**Introduce yourself to
Harlequin Romance Treasury.
The most beautiful books you've ever seen!**

Cover and spine of each volume features a distinctive gilt design.
An elegant bound-in ribbon bookmark completes the classic design.
No detail has been overlooked to make Romance Treasury
volumes as beautiful and lasting as the stories they contain.
What a delightful way to enjoy the very best and most popular
Harlequin romances again and again!

Here's how to get your volume NOW!

MAIL IN	$	GET
2 SPECIAL PROOF-OF-PURCHASE SEALS*	PLUS $1 U.S.	ONE BOOK
5 SPECIAL PROOF-OF-PURCHASE SEALS*	PLUS 50¢ U.S.	ONE BOOK
8 SPECIAL PROOF-OF-PURCHASE SEALS*	FREE	ONE BOOK

*Special proof-of-purchase seal from inside back cover of all specially marked Harlequin "Let Your Imagination Fly Sweepstakes" volumes. No other proof-of-purchase accepted.

ORDERING DETAILS:

Print your name, address, city, state or province, zip or postal code on the coupon below or a plain 3" x 5" piece of paper and together with the special proof-of-purchase seals and check or money order (no stamps or cash please) as indicated. Mail to:

**HARLEQUIN
ROMANCE TREASURY
BOOK OFFER
P.O. BOX 1399
MEDFORD, N.Y. 11763, U.S.A.**

Make check or money order payable to: Harlequin Romance Treasury Offer. Allow 3 to 4 weeks for delivery.

Special offer expires: June 30, 1981.

PLEASE PRINT

Name

Address

Apt. No.

City

State/Prov.

Zip/Postal Code

Let Your Imagination Fly Sweepstakes

Rules and Regulations:

NO PURCHASE NECESSARY

1 Enter the Let Your Imagination Fly Sweepstakes 1, 2 or 3 as often as you wish. Mail each entry form separately bearing sufficient postage. Specify the sweepstake you wish to enter on the outside of the envelope. Mail a completed entry form or, your name, address, and telephone number printed on a plain 3"x 5" piece of paper to:
HARLEQUIN LET YOUR IMAGINATION FLY SWEEPSTAKES,
P.O. BOX 1280, MEDFORD, N.Y. 11763 U.S.A.
2. Each completed entry form must be accompanied by l Let Your Imagination Fly proof-of-purchase seal from the back inside cover of specially marked Let Your Imagination Fly Harlequin books (or the words "Let Your Imagination Fly" printed on a plain 3"x 5" piece of paper Specify by number the Sweepstakes you are entering on the outside of the envelope.
3 The prize structure for each sweepstake is as follows:

Sweepstake 1 – North America

Grand Prize winner's choice: a one-week trip for two to either Bermuda; Montreal, Canada; or San Francisco. 3 Grand Prizes will be awarded. (min. approx. retail value $1,375. U.S., based on Chicago departure) and 4,000 First Prizes: scarves by nik nik, worth $14 U.S. each. All prizes will be awarded.

Sweepstake 2 – Caribbean

Grand Prize winner's choice: a one-week trip for two to either Nassau, Bahamas; San Juan, Puerto Rico; or St. Thomas,Virgin Islands. 3 Grand Prizes will be awarded. (Min. approx. retail value $1,650. U.S., based on Chicago departure) and 4,000 First Prizes: simulated diamond pendants by Kenneth Jay Lane, worth $15 U.S. each. All prizes will be awarded.

Sweepstake 3 – Europe

Grand Prize winner's choice: a one-week trip for two to either London, England; Frankfurt, Germany; Paris, France; or Rome, Italy 3 Grand Prizes will be awarded. (Min. approx. retail value $2,800 U.S., based on Chicago departure) and 4,000 First Prizes: 1/2 oz. bottles of perfume, BLAZER by Anne Klein. (Retail value over $30 U.S.) All prizes will be awarded.

Grand trip prizes will include coach round-trip air-fare for two persons from the nearest commercial airport serviced by Delta Air Lines to the city as designated in the prize, double occupancy accommodation at a first- class or medium hotel, depending on vacation, and $500. U.S. spending money. Departure taxes, visas, passports, ground transportation to and from airports will be the responsibility of the winners.
4. To be eligible, Sweepstakes entries must be received as follows:
Sweepstake 1 Entries received by February 28, 1981
Sweepstake 2 Entries received by April 30, 1981
Sweepstake 3 Entries received by June 30, 1981
Make sure you enter each Sweepstake separately since entries will not be carried forward from one Sweepstake to the next.

The odds of winning will be determined by the number of entries received in each of the three sweepstakes. Canadian residents, in order to win any prize, will be required to first correctly answer a time-limited skill-testing question, to be posed by telephone, at a mutually convenient time.
5. Random selections to determine Sweepstake 1, 2 or 3 winners will be conducted by Lee Krost Associates, an independent judging organization whose decisions are final. Only one prize per family, per sweepstake. Prizes are non-transferable and non-refundable and no substitutions will be allowed. Winners will be responsible for any applicable federal, state and local taxes. Trips must be taken during normal tour periods before June 30, 1982. Reservations will be on a space-available basis. Airline tickets are non-transferable, non-refundable and non-redeemable for cash.
6 The Let Your Imagination Fly Sweepstakes is open to all residents of the United States of America and Canada, (excluding the Province of Quebec) except employees and their immediate families of Harlequin Enterprises Ltd., its advertising agencies, Marketing & Promotion Group Canada Ltd. and Lee Krost Associates, Inc., the independent judging company. Winners may be required to furnish proof of eligibility. Void wherever prohibited or restricted by law. All federal, state, provincial and local laws apply.
7 For a list of trip winners, send a stamped, self-addressed envelope to:
Harlequin Trip Winners List, P.Q. Box 1401, MEDFORD, N.Y. 11763 U.S.A.
Winners lists will be available after the last sweepstake has been conducted and winners determined.
NO PURCHASE NECESSARY

Let Your Imagination Fly Sweepstakes

OFFICIAL ENTRY FORM

Please enter me in Sweepstake No. _____

Please print:

Name _____

Address _____

Apt. No. _____ City _____

State/ Prov. _____ Zip/Postal Code _____

Telephone No. area code _____

MAIL TO:
HARLEQUIN LET YOUR
IMAGINATION FLY SWEEPSTAKE No._____
P.O. BOX 1280,
MEDFORD, N.Y. 11763 U.S.A.
(Please specify by number, the Sweepstake you are entering.)